# A

# SONG

# FROM

# FARAWAY

# A
# SONG
# FROM
# FARAWAY

*A novel*

## Deni Ellis Béchard

MILKWEED EDITIONS

Published 2020 by Milkweed Editions
Printed in Canada
Cover design by Mary Austin Speaker
Cover photograph by Kramer O'Neill
20 21 22 23 24   5 4 3 2 1
*First Edition*

Milkweed Editions, an independent nonprofit publisher, gratefully acknowledges sustaining support from the Alan B. Slifka Foundation and its president, Riva Ariella Ritvo-Slifka; the Ballard Spahr Foundation; *Copper Nickel*; the Jerome Foundation; the McKnight Foundation; the National Endowment for the Arts; the National Poetry Series; the Target Foundation; and other generous contributions from foundations, corporations, and individuals. Also, this activity is made possible by the voters of Minnesota through a Minnesota State Arts Board Operating Support grant, thanks to a legislative appropriation from the arts and cultural heritage fund. For a full listing of Milkweed Editions supporters, please visit milkweed.org.

Library of Congress Cataloging-in-Publication Data

Names: Béchard, Deni Ellis, 1974- author.
Title: A song from faraway : stories / Deni Ellis Béchard.
Description: First edition. | Minneapolis, Minnesota : Milkweed Editions, 2020.
Identifiers: LCCN 2019041216 (print) | LCCN 2019041217 (ebook) | ISBN 9781571311351 (trade paperback) | ISBN 9781571317216 (ebook)
Subjects: LCSH: Masculinity--Fiction. | Identity (Psychology)--Fiction. | Fatherhood--Fiction. | War and society--Fiction. | Psychological fiction.
Classification: LCC PR9199.4.B443 A6 2020  (print) | LCC PR9199.4.B443 (ebook) | DDC 813/.6--dc23
LC record available at https://lccn.loc.gov/2019041216
LC ebook record available at https://lccn.loc.gov/2019041217

Milkweed Editions is committed to ecological stewardship. We strive to align our book production practices with this principle, and to reduce the impact of our operations in the environment. We are a member of the Green Press Initiative, a nonprofit coalition of publishers, manufacturers, and authors working to protect the world's endangered forests and conserve natural resources. *A Song from Faraway* was printed on acid-free 100% post-consumer-waste paper by Friesens.

# A
# SONG
# FROM
# FARAWAY

# I

(1992–2008)
THE UNITED STATES
CANADA
IRAQ

# Kali Yuga

T he first time I met my half brother I was seventeen and he
was fourteen. I had organized my assignments for the trip
and jacketed my textbooks in butcher paper, but when I
arrived at the airport in Virginia and saw the hale blue-jeaned boy
and his mother, as thin and erratic as the menthol 100 she soon lit
up, I knew I should have left my schoolwork behind.

He caught me in a bear hug, his chin against my collar as if he
were going to bite me. Not once that day did his mother address
me directly. She spoke like a poet to the air, "Hot dogs on the table.
Coke in the fridge." The sky was haze and glare, humidity worse
than the drizzle Vancouver's writers so often elegize.

That evening, as he took me to meet two of his friends, he
told me that his mother had named him after the guy who owned
*Playboy* magazine. He announced that he planned to one-up his
namesake, the way a six-year-old might, dumb and proud, point-
ing at his chest with his thumb.

We met his friends (two brothers with beards), and with them
we wandered the lumpy terrain of an incipient subdivision, drank
Busch (hidden suitably in the bushes), and visited an abandoned
Ford Mustang whose tires and windows the duo had blasted with
shotguns (the glass mixed with smashed Jack Daniel's bottles, one
black-and-white label stuck to a seat). I learned that the Mustang

belonged to a family whose many generations sounded as if they were composed of violent brothers, all of whom resided in a single house. Hugh and the beards had some sort of feud with them, and as a result of it, we later fled a red monster truck on lifters (Confederate flag and devil cab lights and hee-hawing passengers). Hugh was the least fearful, standing in the middle of the road as he watched the truck race toward him, his eyes as wide as tunnels. Then he turned, mooned it, and darted into the trees, hooting and monkey-like as he hitched up his jeans.

When he and I arrived back at his house, dawn was a faint, ugly elbow smear on the dark glass of his little town. I supposed I'd been treated as any visitor from afar, regaled by local tradition. I was three years older than Hugh, but next to him I felt young. I didn't understand how our father could have produced two entirely different creatures nor why the second looked so much more like him.

"I'm happy as shit to see you, Andy," Hugh said and hugged me like a wrestler grapples.

"It's Andrew," I corrected, not for the first time that night.

"If you say so," he told me. He then insisted that I sleep next to him, in his bed, his arm around me and his beer snores in my face.

———

The second time we saw each other was at my father's funeral, and it was, Hugh told me, his first trip out of Virginia. He was seventeen, close to graduating and wearing the shoulder-length hair and cropped beard of a country rock star. He'd flown to Vancouver for the death of a man he'd met twice and had paid his way with earnings from working construction, what his high school considered Life Credits and for which it let him out at noon.

"I can't believe it," he told me, hunched as if to confide. "We were gonna travel the country when I finished school. We talked about it."

I glanced away, afraid he'd see his stupidity in my eyes. My father never followed through on his plans or promises. He could talk in a way to make anyone dream, on the rare occasion that he actually conceded to talking—usually after too many drinks. But he was always one novel revision away from having the time to do the things he'd promised. I'd learned this as a boy, though I said nothing to Hugh. I let him squeeze his tears and pay fealty to my mother's mourning, which came from the bitterness of years spent waiting to inherit my father's wealth. Hugh didn't know this, and she received his gesture, not hugging him but extending her hand for him to touch, like a pope with a ring to be kissed.

Afterward, I showed him my father's basement study, rank with BO and two decades of bourbon fumes, cramped with a heaped escritoire and walls of sagging, overflowing bookshelves, the single high window heavily draped. At the center of it all squatted the reading chair whose synthetic nap had been worn to a glassy sheen, its right arm flecked with the burn marks of fallen cigarette embers. I couldn't bring myself to say that my father had had about as much impact on my life as a boarder would have. Instead, I described the three novels he'd published about being a draft dodger, doing my best to make him sound heroic.

"Did he talk about me much?" Hugh asked.

I cleared my throat. The air was thick and musty down there, and I had to clear my throat again. He knew nothing about our father and had no right to care. He stooped, as if the ceiling were too low, and held one arm across his chest, like a spent boxer waiting for the final punch.

"He told me you were like him," I said, lowering my eyes. In front of the chair was a greasy-looking patch of carpet where my father's feet had rested. When he'd told me I had a half brother, I'd asked him how he could be sure Hugh was really his. "The boy's my spitting image," he'd said and then, when he saw my face, added, "Consider yourself lucky."

"Did he leave me anything?" Hugh asked.

"This was his," I told him. A leather jacket lay on the desk, so new it smelled of the tannery. My father had bought it a week ago, the cut immodestly fashionable, unlike anything he'd ever worn. It was the sort of jacket a poorly aging man might go for.

Hugh clutched it, bunching up his shoulders and inhaling. He stared at the shelves, and the way he looked at them made me look too, at the crooked and piled-up spines in the faint, almost particulate light, each book thick with use and broken-backed.

"Maybe," he said, "maybe someday I could be a writer too."

I scrunched up my cheeks as if I might agree.

———

That evening, I introduced Hugh to Nathalie, a love interest, my relationship with her having stalled during a month of platonic outings only to bloom suddenly in the warm climate of my father's death, after a night when I broke down and cried. She brushed aside my discomfort with Hugh's redneck bearing, telling me I should be proud that he looked up to me. We took him to Gastown, the Spaghetti Factory, and the comedy club, where he ignored the jokes and repeatedly asked Nathalie questions.

"So you studied computers?"

"I did my degree in programming."

"That's not building them, is it?"

"No, it's putting the information in. If a computer were a robot, I'd be giving it its personality."

"You know how to do that?"

"Actually, I did my undergraduate thesis in artificial intelligence, but no, I couldn't program robotic AI without a team."

The comic was talking about staying with his fiancée's parents and a toilet with no water in it—the sound the handle made when he hit it repeatedly—and I focused my surprise toward the stage, since I'd had no idea she was interested in artificial intelligence. I knew she'd come to the University of British Columbia from MIT to do graduate work in a lab developing internet gateways. She was telling Hugh about that now, and he kept saying, "I don't get it." So she spoke in his currency—*Tron: Deadly Discs* and *The Terminator*—and he nodded vigorously at her explanations of computers wiring the world together.

"If your nervous system were the internet, this would be Virginia," she told him and pinched one fingertip of his big hand where it lay limp on the table, abandoned by his overworked brain. "And this would be Vancouver," she added, tweaking his earlobe. For the first time that day, he laughed, guffawing like an idiot. The comedian perked up, thinking he finally had an audience, but Hugh was staring at her, his eyes big and still—one-stop, one-size-fits-all sensory organs, doing the hearing and feeling, maybe even the thinking too.

A few nights after Hugh's return home, the phone rang. Nathalie answered.

"It's Hugh," she told me, holding the mouthpiece to her patterned pajama breast.

I fumbled the receiver to my ear.

"Hugh," I said. "What is it?"

"I'm all fucked up, Andy. I'm all fucked up."

"Where are you?" I asked, as if he weren't three thousand miles away. He must have punched the phone because the earpiece pulsed with a hard thump, and touch tones squealed.

"Go to bed," I told him.

"Aw, fuck you," he said and hung up.

Nathalie was watching me.

"Well, tarnation," I told her, "that boy's done gone off the deep end."

"He doesn't talk like that," she said.

She pushed her hair back along her jaw and looked away, reaching to turn off the light.

———

Nathalie must have made an impression: the next time I heard from Hugh was a few weeks later via the internet. He began writing frequent emails, and in them, he didn't sound half so rustic, as if a computer transistor filtered out his roughness. He confessed that emails made him realize how bad his spoken English was—*I mean, how do you write "a whole 'nother" and not sound stupid?* He said he'd been reading Steinbeck and Thoreau, had tried *Moby-Dick* but was working on the earlier stuff, *building my reading muscles for the big one.* He mentioned no longer doing construction since he'd received his *share of the inheritance.* I stared at the email a long time, not sure why I was surprised that he'd received anything at all.

As I got busier over the months that followed his visit, I answered Hugh's emails less frequently. To his sprawling messages, I shot back replies that were basically apologies for not writing more. I finished my undergraduate degree early and launched into a master's in comp lit, convinced I could finish within a year if I did my coursework and thesis simultaneously. All the while, I began to sense Nathalie becoming unfamiliar. We maintained our rituals of meals, movies, and occasional intercourse, but sometimes, when I looked up from my desk, I no longer recognized her. She was the only woman I'd slept with, six years older and so pale her mousy hair appeared shimmering and dark against her skin. She almost matched my height but was fine boned, her wrists like sticks and her extra weight conspicuous given the slightness of her frame. She appeared a well-fed waif and not the child of a Boston Brahmin financier and a Parisian mother.

After first meeting Nathalie, I questioned her willingness to date an undergraduate, and she said that age and maturity didn't necessarily coincide, and that, anyway, I was something of an old man.

"Not quite as sexy as an old soul," I told her.

"No," she agreed. "Anyway, you really like me."

As I embroiled myself in my thesis ("Silence and the Politics of the Dispossessed: Historicizing Dickens") and subsisted on Chef Boyardee, peel-top ravioli, she took up kickboxing and burned off the last of what she called her baby fat. She tried to convince me to come to class with her, but I let my organizational tendencies get the best of me. I can still see myself gesturing vaguely as I explained to her that I wanted to finish academics, make the transition to the job world, and then get involved with hobbies and sports, but not do everything at once.

The evening before my thesis was due, Nathalie and I were coming back from the bus stop, taking turns with the cage of the hamster she'd inherited from a friend who'd gone off to Bolivia. The poor little thing was crouched, watching its wheel spin with a ghostly motion from the momentum of Nathalie's strides. We came around the corner and saw Hugh sitting on the bottom step of our porch.

"Jesus," I said, and before my eyes flashed the thesis pages my professors would scribble with incredulous red. He was already up and belted me with one of his regional hugs so popular in the World Wrestling Federation. He handled Nathalie more gingerly, as if she were pregnant, though he was just trying to get his arms around the cage.

His hair was collar length and casually mussed, no longer a mullet. He looked more textured, more natural, and less purely redneck, though I couldn't yet identify what had changed over the last—I tried to calculate the time—year and a half?

He smiled as if he might yodel and said, "It's just so good to see the two of you!" His constrained voice called to mind a 1950s housewife exclaiming *Isn't that swell!* I considered that this discord might be the result of his inner redneck going head-to-head with his budding computer geek slash bookworm slash bohemian.

As I invited him inside, I asked him about the knit friendship bracelet on his big, suntanned wrist and the copy of *The Sun Also Rises* in his knapsack pocket.

"I mean," I said, "how do those go over with the beards back home?"

He shrugged. "It's just stuff I got on the road."

Thence began the narrative that would last until after midnight, his way of speaking fluctuating, like a car radio caught between stations. His hillbilly rhythms verged upon taut, overdescriptive, even pedantic phrasing that caused him to slow, as a truck might, coming upon deep potholes. "An e-gre-gious wrong turn," he said at one point and blinked, as if reassuring himself.

All the same, he told his story with relish, conveying that he was doing the right thing, seeing the world in the footsteps of Kerouac and Miller and a few others I hadn't read.

"I've been as far south as the Panama Canal, and as far north as Kuujjuarapik, Québec, on the Hudson Bay. I haven't been to Alaska yet, but I figure I'll head up thataway after this little *de*tour." He elbowed me.

Two pages of red ink, take one down, pass it around. My thesis concerns had become a song one sings driving long distances.

Hugh went on to describe states he'd crossed, people he'd met, communes lived on, meals shared. It sounded like a coming-of-age set in the 1960s, clichéd in all its short-lived glory.

"What's the Arctic like?" Nathalie asked.

"In northern Québec, you're so close to the pole the earth is curved, like you're standing on a hill wherever you go. Sometimes there's a clear three hundred and sixty degrees of horizon and thick moss all over the ground. It's like walking on a mattress. The rock shows through the moss here and there, and most of the stones have been rubbed and rounded by the glaciers. I spent a month on an island in James Bay, just beneath the Hudson Bay. I was living with this girl, Mélanie Boudreau from Montréal. She was up there studying bird migrations. She was all alone, and when she saw me in a canoe, she waved me over. She had black, black hair and the greenest eyes. Man, it was like something from *The Odyssey*. I got out of the canoe, and she asked me a bunch of questions in pretty bad English and then told me I should stay with her. So I did. I guess she thought God had sent her a man, except she was the most hardcore atheist I've ever met. We were like Adam and Eve on the northern edge of the earth. The coldest water ever. The sun was so bright and the air—it was thin and cool. Night hardly lasted an hour. And, man, those French girls, they really know what they want."

He laughed and then suddenly turned red, no doubt remembering that Nathalie was half-French.

"Oh, yes we do," she said and reached out and squeezed his meaty forearm.

"You know," I said and feigned a stretch, "it's already eleven. My thesis is due tomorrow."

"Hey. I'm sorry, bro. I shouldn't be distracting you."

The cage was on the table, the hamster racing in its wheel, and Hugh considered it. None of us spoke as Hugh's gaze got vague and unfocused and he finally said, "I took Dad's last name."

"Maybe you'll be the first Estrada to make it to the Playboy Mansion," I told him.

He guffawed and slapped the table, as if nothing on earth could bother him. But what would my father have thought of his last name and hard-won idealism coupled with a reference to the king of smut? In truth, I didn't really know.

"Did you ever tell Nathalie how your mother chose your name?" I asked him.

"No," he said and grinned. "She saw a TV show about how Hugh Hefner lived and decided that if she had a son, he should be smart enough to get the women and live the good life and take what he wanted. Growing up, I always told myself I'd do a hundred times better."

"That's kind of sweet," Nathalie said. "She must really love you."

It occurred to me that they both had Teflon brains, that nothing could upset them.

"You know," Hugh said, "I'm a dual citizen now."

He fished two passports out of his knapsack. He showed me the Canadian one. The picture was proud, his chest and jaw lifted, with an aura of redneck radiance that is pure, dumb vitality.

"I'm gonna wear these passports out," he said.

Nathalie's eyes were big. "I wish I had your courage."

He blushed and bit his lip and pushed up his cheeks and looked away. He was fabulously handsome, and I looked away too. Courage wasn't the right word for selfishly roaming the world in search of trivial pleasures. I asked if he was hungry.

"Damn, I been on the road all day," he said, his accent back in force. "My stomach feels like a hamster wheel spinnin'"—he smiled at Nathalie—"only there ain't no hamster."

She laughed, and I got up to feed him. Nathalie and I ate a bit but mostly watched Hugh destroy the last of my Chef Boyardees and whatever decent foods Nathalie had smuggled in. Sated, he talked until his head balanced on his hand and his eyes drooped.

"Are you tired?" Nathalie asked.

"Nah," he said, "no way." He gave himself a bronco shake. "My face is just falling asleep."

———

Sometime after 3:00 a.m., as I was sneaking into the kitchen for another cup of instant coffee with a shot of maple syrup (my current compromise to remain alert after Nathalie banned me from sucking on sugar cubes), the hide-a-bed creaked in the living room.

"Hey, Andrew, is that you?"

"Yeah," I said.

"How's the thesis coming?"

"It's not at the moment. I'm just getting coffee."

"Well, I kinda wanted to tell you something if you got a minute."

The mattress springs squealed as he sat up, his shoulders and back sloped in outline against the venetian blinds, like a sitting Grendel silhouetted against the paper-thin slits of streetlight. The room smelled of his open knapsack—BO that had mellowed into an earthy, slightly fecal must—and I had the impression of stepping into a lair. My movement activated a white nightlight at the floor. It lit his face and hollowed his eyes.

"There's something I gotta confess," he told me. "You're not gonna like it."

"Oh," I said and sat on a chair. I switched on a lamp. The rugged redneck face I now saw was somehow less daunting than the wild boy he used to be.

He crouched on the floor with his knapsack and took out a book whose pages looked so old they might have been parchment. The spine had fallen off and the stitching was visible—simple and coarse, as if done by hand. A rubber band held the smudged, wordless cover in place. I'd never seen the book before.

"This changed my life," he said. "I'm sorry. I took it from Dad's shelves when you weren't watching. I just noticed it, and I knew from the look of it how special it was. If there was one thing that would connect me to Dad, this was it."

He stared into my eyes, his blue gaze washing inside my head. I'd never noticed this book, but he'd glanced once at the shelf and known. I'd stored the rest of my father's library and notes in long plastic storage bins under my bed, and this one belonged with the others.

"Man," he said, "I can't tell you how surprised I was when I opened it up. I kept it hidden till I was on the plane. It wasn't even in English. But I knew I'd been right about the book because I saw that the author's name was Rafael Maria Estrada. He had the same last name as you and Dad."

"So . . . you have no idea what it's about?"

"Oh, yeah, I've read it. It's called *The Angels Write Poetry with Blood*. I went to Mexico and learned Spanish. I mean, I'd taken Spanish in high school, but I couldn't get past *cómo estás*. But now I've read the book four times already, and I'm gonna keep reading it until every line makes sense."

"What's it about?" I asked, my throat suddenly dry. Here I was finishing a master's degree, and I could barely decode French without the help of a dictionary. He was only twenty, and his life seemed so raw and authentic I could hardly breathe.

"It's about this young guy who's born in Mexico, in a rich and corrupt family, but slowly he realizes there are things worth fighting for. He's so hungry for life. Everything he does, good or bad, is because he's trying to figure himself out. It just made me realize how big the world is."

"I need to get back to my thesis," I told him.

"What about the book? You're not angry?"

I stood and turned to leave. I hesitated at the door.

"Nah. I'm not angry. The name thing is probably just a coincidence."

———

I like to think of being a hippie as transformative, a sort of cultural conduit, a natural transition from redneck to bourgeois, and vice versa. I came up with that a few mornings later when Hugh, after days perusing Dad's books and attempting to initiate discussions with me about the purpose of life, set off for Alaska. He'd done most of the talking, and I'd fended off his questions of our father and what boiled down to rudimentary teleology by telling him I still had coursework to wrap up.

"It's too good to see you for me to want to go," he'd said at the door, no ticket, just an opposable thumb. I briefly considered asking for the book back, but I didn't speak Spanish and nothing would have sounded pettier.

"I'd like to read that book someday," I told him.

"I'll translate it for you," he said. "Maybe we can get it published in English when I'm finished."

He hugged me, and off he went, and with his departure, Nathalie and I began receiving emails with the story of Rafael, a young man born into a powerful political family before the Mexican Revolution. He reinvents himself repeatedly as he seeks an ideal not motivated by personal gain, fear, or animal desire. He craves the power of profound belief—a cause that will give him shape and strength. I wondered if he was in some way related to my father, if we had a history of self-sacrifice for ideals. I'd never really considered where I was going with literary studies. In high school, the students who liked reading seemed of a privileged class, free of the mundanity of applied sciences, close to those great minds who'd lived fully. Above all, we were gifted with verbosity, capable of cutting others down with a few choice words and not having to pay for it because our school was virtually absent of jocks. But recently, one of my university professors, hearing some colleagues and me reminiscing about our high school days, muttered, "Gifted youth make for pointless adults." He'd said it so we could hear, but without looking at us, as if he were deriding a gaggle of catty teenagers.

I'd always assumed I'd someday write a novel. I figured it would happen on its own, when the timing was right, like the deepening of my voice or the sprouting of body hair. But I'd felt no compulsion. I considered Rafael, his resistance to his father, his longing to assert himself upon the order of the world, and wondered whether I would someday wake and find a truth in literature or my life, and be willing to fight. I worked on my studies, telling myself that I would, that my knowledge would reach critical mass and, like an interstellar gas cloud collapsing under its own weight, catch fire.

As I began a PhD, Hugh's emails added up, hundreds of them over the next two years—his translation of Estrada's book rendered a few paragraphs at a time, the writing clumsy and overwrought. The act of translation seemed the only constant in his life. Every five or six months he showed up at my steps a changed human being. He took college classes, for a while wanted alternately to be the next Faulkner or a Wall Street broker. He learned to box in Las Vegas, studied jiu-jitsu in São Paulo, and Krav Maga in Tel Aviv. When he visited and talked about our family origins— wondering whether our father was Estrada's son or grandson or just a relative—his English was sometimes too bookish, at other times Southern and ungrammatical, moving in mysterious waves and fluctuations, like light.

With each season, he seemed to burn through a lifetime of experience. But on his visits, he still searched through our father's books and notes, trying to connect him to Rafael Maria Estrada. I let him, telling myself that I was outsourcing research into my lineage, that maybe I'd learn something interesting—a good story for the post-lecture cocktail parties that doctoral students and professors attended. My mother told me that our father had rarely spoken about his past other than to say he grew up in Colorado and came from an old American military family. I suggested to Hugh that maybe our father had picked up the book because he'd had his last name in common with the author.

Eventually, Hugh headed to Montréal to live with a new girlfriend, Marie-Eve, but when she dumped him, he did a few Toughman fights—maybe because he'd eaten up his inheritance— and then he moved to Mexico. He worked more on his translation and returned to Vancouver with Pilar, a young woman whose high forehead suggested intelligence. They got an apartment together, not far from us, in Kitsilano. She told me that he spoke Spanish at times like a *bandido*, at others like Borges himself, his divided identity chasing him across cultural boundaries.

When Hugh disappeared, Pilar came around a few times, asking if we'd seen him. I went out looking for Hugh with her, taking her to the police station to see if they might know something. I asked her about him, how he was to live with.

"I am too sad to talk about him now," she said and just her accent, the way it stretched the vowels, made her sound sad indeed. "He *iis* never sat*iis*fied. He *iis* in *soo* much pa*yiin*."

That was all I ever got out of her. After two weeks, when rent came due, she returned to Mexico. I no longer received emails or translations from Hugh, but I didn't worry. He'd likely ditched Pilar for another of his wild quests to uncover an unmanned edge of our great continent. And I was right. Eight months later, he showed up again, rail thin. He told Nathalie and me that he'd been living off the coast of Florida, eating raw foods and doing yoga. When I asked about Pilar and why he'd left, he just waved his hand. He'd come to Vancouver to teach yoga, since, having indeed burned through his inheritance money, he needed a job. He said he had to start over, that his attachments had caused him suffering. The only relic of his past was the book, in a large Ziploc freezer bag, with a few silica moisture-absorbing packets, like the ones inside vitamin containers.

"Vancouver," he announced to Nathalie and me over dinner in an Italian restaurant, "is going to be my home from now on."

His accent had almost vanished, and I found myself listening more closely to what he had to say. Now that his coarse Southern affectation was gone, maybe I'd understand who he really was. But for the first time with Hugh, Nathalie had a guarded look, wariness or concern—I couldn't tell which. His gaze was open as always, but the corners of his eyes appeared pinched, with grief or simply fatigue.

"So," she said, "what's the point of yoga? I guess I never really understood."

Almost imperceptible tension gathered around his eyes, conveying no emotion I knew, as if he had facial muscles the rest of us lacked.

"It's about the self, about stripping it away. It removes imprints from the body and therefore from the mind. It's like sanding the marks from old wood. But then you go deeper. You keep stripping away."

"So the goal is nothing?" she said.

"It's giving up all the attachments that constitute the self so you can rejoin pure being."

"Why are you so eager to jettison your self?" I asked and studiously took a long sip of wine.

"It's easiest to give the self over," he continued, "if we dedicate ourselves to something. Parents can give their selves over to their children, or an artist to her art. You sacrifice the self to do it, to really do it and bring something beautiful into the world. A great leader can give her self over. A great soldier. But the final step is giving the self up entirely."

He and Nathalie were leaning forward over the table, staring at each other. A few furrows had appeared on her forehead, like the faint, rudimentary jottings of a protolanguage, and he considered them, as if these were the marks he would wash away to free her.

"I think they forgot the bruschetta," I said and reached again for my wine.

———

One afternoon while Nathalie was kickboxing, I sat at her computer. Fractals unfolded, splitting out from the edges of the screen. She could remain here for hours, ear buds in, her eyes at once focused and relaxed. Her colleagues at the University of British Columbia messaged her and shared files, and she examined web pages or databases or read screens of code as the occasional chat popped up from her friends in Boston. I imagined her opening my computer and searching my emails or documents and wondered what she would find. It was all so academic. Maybe I'd be outraged just to cover my embarrassment at having so little to hide.

I wiggled her mouse. The fractal disappeared, revealing a dozen layered windows. The foremost was a discussion of malware and spyware. The few paragraphs I read were more interesting than I expected, the tone at once punchy and technical, faintly impatient. I wondered what else lay beneath all these windows. I sat until the screen went dark and the fractals returned.

That week, after Hugh was refused at a dozen yoga studios, he took a job at an adult video club, working the night shift, and a few days later, as Nathalie and I watched TV, the two airliners—clip after played-back clip—repeatedly struck the World Trade Center. I dropped in on Hugh, and he was at the counter, eating cold pizza and reading Bukowski, his Southern accent back like a case of strep. His eyes were different—entranceways into something abandoned.

I didn't know what to say to him. I didn't know what to say to Nathalie either. She'd become addicted to the news. All of us had. In my graduate department, waiting around the microwave, a few of the more outspoken among us ventured that the Americans had it coming, what with their strong-arm politics and military support for extractive industries. But those who said this looked afraid. Nathalie did too, though beneath her fear there seemed to be grief, an air of sad expectation like that of a person whose loved one lay in a distant hospital.

Hugh was harder to read, so, over dinner one night, I asked where he was going with his life. He hesitated, downcast, almost fragile. Like an old shirt that keeps its smell no matter how many times you wash it, his redneck self clearly survived the scourging and ablutions of yoga.

"Nothing expresses all of me," he said softly, with those rolling American vowels. "It's like in Nietzsche's *Birth of Tragedy*, the division between form and chaos . . ."

"Well," I told him, "there's more to philosophy than pop-psychology." If he'd studied Nietzsche in an academic setting, he would know this.

"I never found my voice," he said and stared at me. He had so many faces, but all of them had this openness, this pleading, hungry gaze. "I got all these pieces but nothing to hold them together."

He didn't mention the attacks. Nor did he make any effort to search me out in the weeks to come.

———

Change, or my desire for it, arrived almost suddenly, the way I imagined a man might look in a mirror and realize he's gone gray. My doctoral program in comparative literature felt like a remote one-lane road winding endlessly through low country at a slow and steady pace. To supplement my income, I taught a literature class at a private high school. I started Tai Chi, and though I acted as if I did so at Nathalie's insistence, I found prostatitis to be a more compelling reason. My doctor diagnosed the cause as poor diet, lack of exercise, and too much sitting. I felt the stagnation, a heaviness in my gut, weighing on my hips.

For years, I'd felt I was waiting on something. I had thought that starting a doctorate would change this, but the academic work felt like the intellectual version of day labor—tasks but no vision or purpose. I'd long ago accepted that I had no compulsion to artistic creation. My inner world felt too neat and clean, the way an immaculate room inspired no story.

I decided that commitment and arduous conjugal tasks could give me purpose, a sense of vigor, and a shape to my life. I pictured myself a handyman in my own home, sanding floors, repairing balusters, newels, and mullions (words whose objects I had yet to identify), or reading Milton to a rocking crib. So I proposed to Nathalie.

"You're bored," she said. We were in a café of hardwood and rattan and shady, recessed ambiance, a place now swaying like a houseboat. I felt sick. I hadn't made a fancy occasion of the

proposal because, even after five years, I feared rejection. I had to
be at the café anyway, for a weekly school-sponsored reading, and
having arrived early with her, I felt safe and, admittedly, a little
bored. Marriage had come up like the weather.

"I want passion," she said, her voice reaching me as if through a
funnel, starting loud and finishing whispered. "I don't want to get
married because we've nothing better to do."

I considered the terror of starting over, struggling through
messy firsts, making a relationship fit—of never again witnessing
Nathalie's growing self-appreciation, the way she stood tiptoe in
her underwear and admired her taut kickboxer's legs in the bathroom mirror.

"I love you," I whispered across the table.

"You're bored," she hissed back. "And by the way, your brother
called and wants to see you. He sounded depressed. I told him to
meet us here."

"Great. Right from the very heart of iniquity."

"Well, maybe *we* should rent some of those videos," she said, a
little too loudly.

By the time he got there, one of my students, her hair flopped
to the side and Kool-Aid purple for the occasion, was at the po-
dium reading terse, monotone considerations on suicide. The previous reader had gotten on her knees to beseech humankind to let
their hearts dance the clear-cuts back to life. A boy had accompa-
nied her on the bongos.

"Hey," Hugh said, his face heavy, the skinny yogi vanquished
by Domino's and smut. He was tight around the nostrils, but the
*V* of concern on his brow disappeared when he saw Nathalie. He
smiled and pulled out a chair and squeezed her knee with genuine
affection.

"Ooh, that feels good," she said. "You should give massages."

He withdrew his hand and tipped a look at me. "What's up, bro?"

"What's up, what's up?" I said with apathy more distilled than the water he used to drink.

He stared in that way of his, wide and unshuttered, the way a dog's gaze can seem to absorb the light.

"I was thinking we could talk," he said.

"Yeah?"

"I kind of need to talk."

"Don't we all."

"You okay?"

"Sure."

Just then one of my students came over to me and confessed he was reading Eliot, or rather that he didn't understand it. The girl, with the single long purple bat wing on her head, was reciting, "And they'll find me / sapped dry / like a potted plant / after the vacations."

As I discussed Eliot's crisis and the girl onstage evoked her own, Hugh struck up a conversation with Nathalie, who listened, leaning close, hair curtaining her as if to keep me from seeing how she pinched her earlobe and stared at him in his own canine way. He sounded more natural than usual, more relaxed, and I tried to follow his story despite my student's questions of mermaids in Prufrock and why the narrator would wake from his dreams and drown. Hugh told Nathalie about a time when he was living in Florida and had rowed out to an old lookout stand on a marshy island. He meditated and fasted there for five days, and on the fourth, a small plane passed, saw him, and began circling, the pilot thinking he was stranded.

"I kept waving him away. I didn't need to be rescued, and he finally left. Then I went to leave and discovered I was too weak to row. It took me almost a day to get home."

He tossed his head and laughed, briefly his old self again.

I got up as if to go to the restroom and instead stepped outside, into the rainy city that visitors can find hard to love but that—with its streetlights illuminating amber clouds of drizzle, its wet avenues streaked with taillights, and its sparkling, humid dark filling everything—can give you the feeling that the world is being washed away. I've heard it said Vancouver is the place you go to forget, to start over, to be anything, the California of Canada. I'd never really thought about why my father had come here, never asked him much, but I knew more about him than Hugh ever would. For Hugh, that sad simple past of a defeated man would be something else: a story leading back into the immensity of history—an epic in which he would find his answers.

As a child, hearing my father's stories from time to time, I believed him to be a great man, destined to write books that would change the world. But then I'd come to realize that through his words he was forestalling my disappointment in him, teaching me to believe there was a reason for his absence, that his retreat not only from our family but also from society had meaning. Hugh would never feel how solitary our father had been, how embittered he was that everyone had so easily forgotten the Vietnam War, which, though he refused to fight in it, had defined him. He lived, writing and publishing his novels, and yet, in all of them, rewriting the same book about draft dodgers, working out that conflict so passionately that he seemed to love nothing else and no one. In their pages, he renounced his country over and over—the decisive act of his life.

In the gusty, cloudy night, in the absence of the usual celestial glimmer—no stars, no distant mountain lights of ski resorts or highways like bright ladders in the sky—I walked until whatever I'd felt was rinsed, until I was on my steps and soon undressed and asleep. I woke only to hear the front door open, the hushed exchange of goodbyes, but nothing else of Nathalie's long approach to my unlit bed.

After Hugh left, Nathalie told me he'd enlisted. He was gone more than two years without a word. Enlisting was what he'd wanted to discuss with me. He felt that his country needed him, she said. Maybe he felt that she would understand, both of them being American citizens.

Briefly I pictured him confiding in me and how we might have talked about the changing world, a story I could have related to my colleagues. They'd have listened gravely, nodding, none of them knowing anyone so close to the heat of things, to the history unfolding on our TV screens. Of course, the daydream was self-serving. I don't even know what I would have said. I tried to picture my own nodding gravitas, but I'd probably have lectured him on how wrong the war was. Hugh had no understanding of the big picture. His patriotism was a knee-jerk reaction, at best. It made sense that he'd stopped translating, that he'd given up his literary and beatnik ambitions; the redneck had risen like a swamp thing from his soul and taken its place, prompting him onto the most redneck of paths. Nothing I could have done would have changed that. Later, I might have thought about him more, or feared for him when the war in Iraq started and Afghanistan rarely appeared on the news, but my relationship with Nathalie had become too difficult for me to worry about Hugh.

"I think I need some time alone," she told me one night in April. She'd made a chicken stir-fry for dinner. We'd eaten, and I'd just finished the dishes.

"Sure," I said. "Just tell me when works best for you."

"I mean, I think I should move out for a while."

I'd been wiping down the counter. I leaned against it.

"What are you saying?"

"I need some space. I need to get some distance on us."

"What do you need distance for? We're doing great."

"We're in a rut."

"We just need to think about the next step."

"Maybe I want to move back to Boston."

"Seriously? I mean, every liberal American is applying for immigrant status to Canada. Boston must be a ghost town."

She didn't smile.

"Maybe we should talk this through. You've been doing the same job for as long as I've known you. What do you think the next step for you is?"

"Moving out. Being alone. Getting some space."

"Are you doubting us that much? I felt that we were on the verge of taking—"

"I know. The next step. But we're not. We've been stuck for as long as I can remember."

And then I saw her roller bag and backpack by the door, her laptop case. It was such a cliché, and I was stunned that I hadn't noticed them until now.

I'm not sure I heard much of what she explained next, that she'd sublet the place of a friend who'd gone off to do consultancy in Silicon Valley.

She left quietly, as if just catching an evening flight, her long dark jacket on, her backpack on her shoulder. She drew out the handle of the roller bag and paused, glancing to where I stood across from her, the couch between us and my hands on its back. Outside, rain gusted past a streetlight. She lifted her hand, showing her palm, and then turned and closed the door behind her.

I paced through the house. I shut off the lights, hesitating at each one, as if there were something I still wanted to do in that room.

———

One sleepless night a month later, I got up and switched on a lamp.

Under the bed were the four plastic storage bins that held my father's books and notes. I slid them out and opened them. The smell of must and decay and the stale tobacco smoke that had impregnated the paper filled the room.

I closed my eyes and put my knuckles to my forehead and pressed them there hard. Maybe on a good night he'd join us for dinner, climbing the stairs in one of the bathrobes he'd always worn and that my mother replaced for him every Christmas.

"How's it coming, boy?" he'd ask me, his gray hair frazzled about his head, broken red veins on his swollen face. I'd talk about school, maybe about a book report, and he'd huff and shake his head and almost smile. He did that often when I talked. It reminded me of how the cool kids acted when I answered questions in class.

Most nights, when I was already in bed, I'd hear him leave the basement and turn the microwave on without opening it to see what my mother had left for him. Some days, after school, I'd sit and read by his basement door. My mother didn't like him much, so I told myself I didn't like him either. But when I heard him get up from his chair, its springs creaking, my heart tossed about in my chest. Wanting to run, I put my ear to the wood. His feet shuffled to the bathroom only he used. I listened, as if the sound of his piss hitting the water, the clacking toilet handle, and the flushing mattered in some way.

Were there clues in his books, not just to link two Estradas by their name, but to who he was—whether he'd loved my mother when they'd met, whether he'd seen me as more than the seal on their arrangement: he paying the bills, flush with his family's old money, while my mother kept the house and excelled in her career as an academic editor? I wondered what he would have thought of the man Hugh was becoming, of his adventures and literary ambitions and his decision to enlist. My father had spent his life denouncing state violence, and yet I felt that—though he'd never have admitted it—he would have admired Hugh's choice.

I took out his third novel, A Song from Faraway, about an anti-war musician whose name, like my father's, was Joe, and whose songs no longer mean anything to anyone. Joe ages poorly in his enthusiasm, growing increasingly angry at a world obsessed with materialism, with new wave and glam rock.

Page after page, I saw how the narrator misses the United States, how he studies his conviction. Even after President Carter pardons the draft dodgers, he doesn't return. In his mind, it is the United States that needs the pardon.

When I was a teenager, I found his novels at the public library, not telling him or my mother. I recalled this book most clearly for a scene that I read over and over with titillation: his encounter with an eighteen-year-old girl from rural Virginia.

He has just played to a half-empty bar. The men, who've come to British Columbia for the forestry boom, have their backs to him, drinking and talking or shooting pool as he strums songs that would have elicited cheers and chants only a few years before. He meets the girl just as she's coming in the door, as he's leaving with his guitar case.

"Hey," she says, and immediately, from the way she smiles, he knows she wants something. "I need gas money to get home," she tells him.

"Where's home?"

"Virginia."

"I'll help you," he says. He has it in his head both to go with her and pay the way, and to convince her that she should stay, that life is better here. He buys her a drink and food, and he keeps promising to give her money for the road. She tells him she's on her way back from Alaska where her father went to work on the pipelines.

She stays with him in a motel, in North Vancouver, and for five days, he doesn't tell anyone where he is—doesn't call the woman he's been living with, the mother of his son.

Maybe my father made the scene up. I vaguely recalled my mother reporting his absence, in the same way Pilar had when I'd gone with her to the police station after Hugh's disappearance.

In the novel—if that's what it was—my father tells the girl his story, but she doesn't get it. She's tall and thin and full of reckless youth and so hungry for sex it feels like a fight. Everything about her, the way she drawls or smokes, her assumptions and prejudices, turn him on. But gradually the scene makes clear that this encounter is nothing special for her. She just wants to outdrink, outfuck, outfight the father who abandoned her, and even as my father tries to make her understand his convictions, she's cracking a can of beer or straddling him again in bed. Her two older half brothers went to Vietnam, and she doesn't care to hear cowardice and bravery redefined. One morning, when he comes back from the 7-Eleven with a fresh stock of beer and cigarettes and chips, her car is gone.

Reading the scene again, I longed for Nathalie. I hated Hugh. I blamed him for no reason I could explain—for Nathalie's absence, for my father's distance. There were too many people in my head, too many emotions. It was ridiculous, that the scene of Hugh's conception was turning me on, that the naked, eager, menthol-thin body of his mother could inhabit my father's world of literary obsessions more fully than my academic mother or I ever had. The book's narrator had "a son." This was told in passing, the way one might offhandedly confess to a failure or weakness—a shirked, unwanted obligation.

Hugh must have read these novels too, though he never mentioned them to me. He probably thought I'd ignore him or tell him that they were just novels. Who else did he have in his life to talk to? He cc'd Nathalie with the translations of *The Angels Write Poetry with Blood*. Maybe he'd written her other messages. I vaguely recalled her mentioning that she'd answered questions he had about the internet and computers, how he sometimes needed help researching his passion du jour. I feared that they were still in touch and she'd told him that she'd left me. I no longer knew if I should envy his missions, his need for a quest, or if he was even still alive.

April, May, June, the Iraq War hogged the news. I went to the gym every day, to Tai Chi three times a week. I watched movies when I couldn't sleep.

Nathalie never made up her mind about Boston. She hurt her knee kickboxing, and loneliness got the better of her. She began sleeping over, and those first summer days were long and vivid. We made love often. I gave her massages. We ordered in, ate out. I bought a sushi roller and learned to cook. We didn't talk about our relationship until a weekend when we rode the ferry to Nanaimo and swam off the small rocky islands along the coast.

The sun was setting, the water darkly luminous, its surface like a mirror in an unlit room. Nathalie was watching the horizon, her back to me, her hair twisted into a bun. Her neck appeared slender and regal, and I wanted to kiss the curve of her shoulder.

"How come you never moved back to Boston?" I asked.

She didn't look at me, and I barely made out her words.

"Because then it would have been over."

I turned in the water with the motion of the waves—the dark, wet, jumbled rocks of the shore, and the trees above; the dim water to the east beyond which lay Vancouver—and back to Nathalie. She was facing me now, a single sun freckle dark beneath the corner of her eye, strangely visible in the half-light, like the imprint of a tear.

"Will you come back to Boston with me?" she asked.

I moved my hand over my face as if to wipe away water. I nodded. I glanced just past her, at the light. I said, "Okay."

She paddled close and wrapped her legs around me. She put her head to my shoulder.

I'd never felt so wanted. I kissed her neck even as I sank slightly, salt stinging my eyes with each wave, getting in my nose. There were moments when I couldn't help but think that if I'd been someone different, if I'd somehow prepared and made myself more ready and worthy, the moment I was in would have been perfect. Then I would have held her afloat with ease. But we had only a few minutes until the stress of treading water for two got the better of me. She let go just as I began to pant. We swam to shore, and there, clambering on the rocks, I asked—as if I'd failed the moment and wanted to prove it by ruining it completely—whether she'd heard from Hugh.

"No," she said, her eyes distracted, bothered by the sunlight against the water. I almost asked again, but I didn't want to risk our happiness.

———

It was in a Boston restaurant, two months later—after I arranged to finish my doctoral dissertation at a distance, took a job as a substitute high school teacher, and moved into an apartment in Cambridge with Nathalie, near Central Square—that I proposed again. For the first time, we'd found a harmony in shared activity, in changing cities together, in choosing a neighborhood and a place that we painted and furnished. But for me there was always the lingering question of what would happen when we had nothing else to do and fell back on old ways. So I planned the proposal, each element, including myself—gym-fit and tanned from a carefully observed quota of hours outdoors. I researched marriage proposals online, learned how to select a ring, reserved dinner flambé in a place where people knew to bow from the waist, tipped the evening's violinist beforehand to strategically wring out his heart.

"On one condition," Nathalie said that night in the restaurant, romance fluttering off like sparrows around a kicked soccer ball. Other patrons were watching, murmuring, fluttery themselves, and I wished the hard ball of her voice would scatter them too, or else that she'd be happy, however briefly.

"What?" I whispered, on my knees, gripping the table as if begging for food.

The violinist, a dapper Vietnamese American man, had his eye on us. I expected dulcet tones—mood music—but he began to move his arm violently, the rising waves of sound giving me the impression that I'd accidentally purchased tragedy, not romance. He played as if Agamemnon were about to sacrifice his daughter in exchange for fair winds to Troy. I'd given him a hundred, so maybe he wanted to prove he'd earned it.

Nathalie hesitated, scanning the room, taking stock of the people watching us, and briefly—I wasn't sure I was seeing this right—there was fear in her eyes. She seemed to shake with self-restraint, hunched up on herself like a cornered animal.

"That you take risks," she said.

Each time neither of us spoke, the violinist jammed in trills or crescendoed, and each time he noticed our lips moving, he dropped to near silence, though he occasionally punctuated our words by plucking a string. I wanted to take the wine bottle to the son of a bitch's head.

"Okay, okay, okay," I lipped as subtly as possible and gestured, and the muscles of her face pulled in different directions. A smile began to take shape, and I think I heard sighs of relief at the nearest table. She started to speak, and the violin fell toward silence, and I knew we'd reached the eye of this musical hurricane, that this was the word I'd been waiting for.

"And you have to take sexual counseling with me," she said.

"Yes," I told her and moved to fit the ring onto her finger. The violinist's bow jerked on the strings, a spasm of sound I couldn't believe was intentional, unless avant-garde. She drew her hand back, pushing the ring the rest of the way, staring at it as if with caution—as if it were the first step in a highly experimental and risky medical treatment.

The violinist regained control and once again started his climb. He plateaued with one interminable note as if beyond this moment the story were over and there was nothing else.

It came to me then that she might be saying there was something wrong with our lovemaking.

"Yes," she said.

But the question had long left me, and I had no idea what she was talking about.

———

There's probably some part of our brains that's smarter than we are. Millions of years of evolution—of hunting and danger, competition for food and sexual rivalry—selected for this. While the dumb self sits at the campfire, bragging or flirting or shoveling in food, the command center is churning information: every glance and gesture around us, every potential tool and weapon, every shift in the mood, in weather, in conversation.

I had a sense of impending change. If I were an ancient shepherd, I might have expected raiders from the hills, at the very least wolves. My solar plexus ached. Deep behind my eyes—a tightening knot of apprehension. Maybe ancient prophets were simply the ones who could feel their intuition fully—never obscuring it with dissonant thoughts of how they wanted the world to be—and then translate it into words. Maybe, as Hugh had described, they knew how to let the self fall away.

It was Hugh I had on my mind: a sense that I would see him soon. I pictured that cartoon redneck waiting outside, behind a lamppost. Ever since my visit to Virginia years ago, he'd lived in my memory as if sketched in the panel of a comic strip: his eyes bulging, his face lit up with awe and enthusiasm as the monster truck raced close. But no matter how I remembered them, Hugh and his friends remained inaccessible: jungle headhunters in loincloths, me the baffled white man. Why did some Americans crave purpose so badly? Why did they believe it was their lot to change the world, often for the worse, though they claimed to be saving it?

Only a few weeks had passed since my engagement to Nathalie. I was sitting before her computer again, in a different room this time, a different city and country. In an age when security is de rigueur, she didn't even have a password—at least not here, at home. I couldn't say what she did to protect herself from the world at large.

I opened her inbox. There was his name. I found it hard to breathe. Over and over: Hugh Estrada. I clicked to her earliest emails and then went to the place, eight years ago, when he came into our lives. There were just a few of his messages back then, many of them the same that he'd sent me, with the exception of his questions to her about the internet, clearly announced in the subject lines: *can emails get lost in the mail?* or *does somebody keep track of everywhere I go on the internet?* I didn't open them. I wouldn't invade her privacy; I was proud of not being that kind of person.

I scrolled through her inbox, through the period when he began sending the translations to both of us, and I considered *The Angels Write Poetry with Blood*, that story of Rafael's self-transformation and discovery, and of Hugh's.

Where his emails to me had dropped off—the time of his enlistment, of my first proposal to Nathalie: a simple calculation that I struggled with, my brain balking, suddenly exhausted—they continued to her. Clusters of emails were punctuated by periods of silence, but these lulls in correspondence became shorter with each passing month, from a few weeks to a week, to a few days, to now, more recently, no more than a day or two. Each time I saw his name, my pulse thudded in my ears, so that the increasing pace of their correspondence came to me as an accelerating soundtrack, reminiscent of the theme to *Jaws*.

I was sweating hard. I got up from my chair and paced the apartment, looked in the rooms, out every window. My lungs kept grabbing at the air.

I hurried back to the computer and opened a recent email. It was a translation from *The Angels Write Poetry with Blood*, a piece of the story I recognized from years ago, about Rafael falling in love with a woman whose social class was the enemy of his ideals—a hackneyed trope but retranslated, the sentences taut and evenly paced, Hugh's control over the language at once muscular and delicate. I read Nathalie's response as well—*I never fully realized until now how similar Rafael's journey is to your own, how much you have both examined yourselves and taken risks to learn and grow, knowing that you could fail and lose everything.* I went back and reread his translation, no longer hearing the guffawing cartoon redneck but a clear voice—that of a man at once assured and determinedly self-doubting, intent on the object of his love even though he knew he could never have her.

———

I was hurrying to the first class of a week-long course (The Path to Ecstasy: Tantra and Sexual Liberation), jogging to catch the T, when I heard Hugh call my name. I just stopped and turned, as if only days had passed since I'd last seen him.

He had the tanned, lined face of a military man who has seen too much, and was sitting on a bench, derelicts and drug addicts on either side, this being Central Square. He looked stern and clean-cut, like a soldier from a war long ago.

"Hugh," I said. At that moment, when I was struggling to throw plot, climax, and denouement all at once into my love life—my first test now awaiting me in a Pilates studio sublet for group therapy—I knew I should make this encounter as short as possible. I was sweating. The street glistened. Heat lines rose, blurring the air like fumes, as if the world were drenched in gasoline and any word I might speak would ignite it.

He stood and came toward me slowly, his eyes moving in careful increments—taking in my posture, trying to determine whether I might hug him or hit him or simply walk right past him. When I did nothing but stand there, he shook my hand.

"I've been wanting to talk to you for a long time," he said.

Through a grate at our feet came the chiming of the T passengers inserting their cards. Metal wheels screeched on the rails, and hotter air billowed up beneath me as the train arrived.

"Yeah," I managed to say, "we've been long overdue for a good catch-up."

"Nah," he said. "I mean, we should really talk, about real things." I just nodded.

"There's so much going on in the world," he told me, softly, his eyes searching to the only available distance, at the end of Mass Ave. "These aren't good times. No one's willing to face it. If we want to survive, we have to reinvent ourselves."

I didn't think he'd come to discuss politics, and the tone of his words was at odds with his military face.

"Did you finish translating the book?" I asked.

"Yeah. I don't think I ever sent you the ending. I found something about Estrada on the internet recently, a web page about him. It says he moved to the United States at the end of his life and stopped writing, so maybe he is related to Dad."

The train rumbled away beneath us, the sidewalk vibrating. I gave him my cell number and offered to meet after my class, not thinking of course that Nathalie might expect me to practice what we'd learned.

"All right, brother," he said as if we'd just finished a long, hard task, as if I'd been to war with him. He half-lifted his hand even as he was turning away.

On the subway platform, I stared at the tracks. A Starbucks cup and a sodden copy of the *Phoenix* lay between them. I tried to quell panic. What did I hope to achieve with Nathalie? Marriage had become an artificial structure, cleanly evacuated in the postmodern age. Endings no longer gave us meaning, nor was there a universal definition for happiness. At least that's what I'd come to believe after years reading critical theory and cultural studies. Though I'd never felt the urgency Hugh did, maybe humans were hardwired with a need for story, and I was failing because of my lack of quest.

I hadn't even fought to be on time for sex therapy. I was becoming a masochist, a fanatic, the Rambo of failure.

When I arrived, ten couples and Nathalie stood at a buffet, watching pornography—a close-up of penetration. Their faces showed a clear loss of appetite, the food in their hands held like fish guts. The teachers, a skinny asexual couple, were rocking on their heels with pleasure, and I learned that the program had started with an informal talk, then the buffet, and that the TV, positioned nearby, had been turned on halfway through the meal and cocktail chatter—*in medias res*, as the critics say—of a heated sex scene. Afterward, we discussed our responses. The couples were mostly administrative types, the exceptions being a stately attorney and his blond figurehead, a tall Haitian man of indeterminate age and his unaffected doctor wife, and Nathalie. Most admitted to shock or arousal, and when it was my turn, I said, "I felt really guilty," not because I meant it, but because I didn't want to sound like everyone else, and besides, an extreme scene merited an extreme response on the basis of literary standards. Everyone looked at me, and the teachers hummed and twiddled their fingers like villains. The discussion then turned to more scientific things, diagrams of reproductive organs, the controversy of the G-spot, angles of entry, glands and lubrication and pressure points.

"Pretty dry," the woman teacher punned, and we all went, "Uh-huh."

"You see, sex starts with your feelings," she said and elaborated the way a magician unfolds a handkerchief into a parachute. Had we signed up not for the 101 but the 001 class, remedial sex, no credits offered, pass/fail only? My peers did not seem dysfunctional at this level. She told us we had to start with the basics, and that later we would learn wild things: the poetry of postures, diving crane, tiger and gazelle, knotted snakes, bee on the stamen. Her androgynous and interchangeable partner was now distributing questionnaires.

"Take these to your corners," he said, "and fill them out in total honesty."

We were given pens. We answered the questions: threesome, foursome, anal sex, preferences, fantasies, infidelities. Then the pens were taken away. Men and women were made to line up against opposite walls, the way we'd done at elementary school dances before the teachers picked partners.

"Now," said one of the instructors as rolls of tape were passed around, "attach the questionnaires to your chest and go and let everyone read them. I want you all to read them and then look the person in the eye and focus on accepting—not forgiving, because that implies something wrong was done. Just accept."

I taped and roamed, and no one appeared impressed by the others' sheets until I saw the stately attorney reading Nathalie's and nodding gravely, as if to say this was a case he wasn't likely to take. She was staring at me from across the room, blushing, her eyes glassy with fear or shame. She strode from the attorney and let me read. She had a lot of little ticks and checks absent on my own sheet and, given the focus here on record keeping, I couldn't see why they shouldn't be dated. Then I read the last one. *Have you been unfaithful to your significant other?* I didn't look her in the eyes. We returned to our walls. The instructors brought folding dividers to screen off the women as if, now that we'd been overwhelmed with regret, it was time for synagogue.

The light from the big studio windows was muted by the division, evening sudden and atilt and ceremonious. The instructors explained the first ritual of acceptance, the apparition of the woman not with her earthly baggage but as goddess.

"This is the dance of Shakti," Instructor A said solemnly, as if addressing the audience at an avant-garde theater. "The woman comes to you as the primal female force. Men tend to be closed and limited, and their judgment is severe. It is only by accessing her true power that a woman can become free. Today we will learn this. The women must lead. Tomorrow, the men will perform the dance of Shiva."

I grimaced and clenched as one by one the women were made to leave the screen and dance for us, awkward in business skirts and blouses, all of them earnest and embarrassed and with a predilection for Indian hand gestures and a gyrating of the body common to hula dancers.

Then Nathalie stepped out, fierce and red in the face. Lilies and orchids and roses had been set in pots, incense lit on brass plates and smoking from the stipples on pyramids, the cardinal directions marked with lavender mantles. She moved and twisted, Martha Graham and Twyla Tharp and Mary Wigman. I'd never seen her like that. She finished with an entreaty, staring at me, crouching and moving her arms as if pulling a chain. The Haitian man gave me a wide look of envy and amazement, and I stood and fled the smoky fragrance into the cool and empty night.

———

Hugh's arrival, as it turned out, was timely. Tonight was clearly not destined for a practice session. We walked the waterfront without speaking. I wanted to find some hint of his innocence in his face so that I could speak, but I couldn't look at him.

"I have to do the dance of Shiva tomorrow," I said just to break the silence, hoping that my words would lead to him speaking about Nathalie in such a way that I could determine his guilt. "Who is Shakti anyway? I'm Shiva. Isn't Kali Shiva's wife?"

"It's not so simple," he told me and sighed as if relieved to talk about something so abstract. "Shakti is a god's wife, mainly Shiva's. She's female energy. But she has two sides. Destructive and creative. Kali and Parvati."

We were briefly silent, looking out at the water.

"That's what I want to talk about," he said. "That's exactly it."

I turned sharply, and he seemed incalculably old and tired. I had the impression that despite his many selves, this was the real Hugh, lean and military, weathered like a rock, and that whatever he shared now would be the truth.

"The changes we are seeing in the world were predicted millennia ago," he said. "We are living in the Kali Yuga."

This wasn't about Nathalie. I couldn't make sense of how his words related to Shakti and I told him so.

"The Kali Yuga is the age of darkness in the Hindu calendar, the machine age, the time when we are farthest from God. The prophets say this will be an age of chaos and madness."

He looked at the sky as if a great flaming ball had lit the night, though there was just an airplane leaving Logan, passing high above with a reedy slip of air. I couldn't tell if the inane talk was to hide his guilt or if he was becoming a spooked, war-ruined vet.

"Haven't people always been crazy?" I asked.

"Not like this."

I tried to picture Nathalie's face the day after he walked her home from the café. I couldn't remember his face from earlier that night. I had the sense that I'd never known him. I felt certain that if I read Nathalie's inbox, I would find the entire miraculous history of his life that I had always refused to hear, or some version of hers that she hadn't shared with me.

He glanced at my eyes and hesitated. "I have a book coming out."

I turned to him, failing to hide my surprise.

"It's a collection of blogs. I wrote them about the war. A memoir, I guess . . . But I know it's a cop-out. It's not real literature."

I shook my head slightly, as if I disagreed.

"Remember after Dad died," I said, "and you told me you wanted to be a writer?"

I tried to speak the words as if I were proud, as if I'd believed in him all along.

"I always knew what you thought of me," he said.

"What?"

"I was some dumb redneck trying to steal your father from you. Let's just get it out."

"I don't know what you're talking about."

"Aw, you fucking coward," he said, but not with rage. He was still staring at the sky, as if he weren't arguing with me at all. I kept silent, ready to wait this out.

"I made a promise to myself," he told me. "I wasn't going to be afraid of anything. I read Dad's books. I saw how much he'd invested in one big idea. He was afraid to change, to let go of that idea so he could live the life he wanted. Meeting you and learning about him, and reading and translating Estrada, I realized that the self is pretty much just an idea, or a mix of ideas. So I kept pushing its boundaries to see who I really was or who I could become."

I still didn't speak. I had questions, but I wasn't sure I wanted to hear their answers. Unlike him, I'd never needed to test my limits since I'd been trained to believe that—theoretically speaking at least—there were none. The permutations of identity were infinite but not absolute, and to change oneself without a culturally determined goal was a quest toward nothingness. Maybe in the process of searching for a truth beyond himself—one he couldn't break— he'd tried on my life like he had so many others.

"Social categories don't work anymore," he said. "Look at us, here, together, brothers."

I wanted to tell him that categories had never been simple for millions of humans throughout history: Persians mixing with Alexander the Great's people; the Gauls watching Roman fathers and brothers leave with the army. But all I could picture was *Asterix* comic books, the puny Romans and the hearty, magical, and defiant Gauls.

As if reading my mind, he said, "I should have been just another oafish country boy. I still think about how much I loved working construction and hanging out with my friends and the high school girls at the Sumerduck racetrack on Saturdays and sneaking beers."

"I don't remember my visit to Virginia as pastoral bliss."

He looked at me and for the first time I saw hostility.

"Do you ever go home?" I asked, ratcheting my voice down to a near whisper.

"My mother died when I was with Pilar. That was the last time."

"That's why you went to Florida?" I asked, and he nodded.

I couldn't remember much about his mother, just that she was a tall, thin woman whose indifference to me I'd found frightening. I thought of the scene in my father's novel, her hunger for contact, for life, and how she'd named her son after Hugh Hefner, intent on offering him, despite her limited knowledge, a symbol of greatness.

The water was almost still, the tide a slight ebb, and the city preserved us in the impression of endless dusk as he started his story all over again, how he met me, how after our father's funeral nothing satisfied him anymore. He'd gotten his GED, traveled, fought, loved women, and been educated but never belonged. I thought of all the times he'd visited, always different, as if he'd come to see me simply so I could affirm him. But I couldn't recall having been faced with anything other than affectations, the burly husks of obsolete archetypes.

"Whenever I was stepping outside of myself, even outside of a new self I had recently become," he said, "that's when I felt sane."

"Maybe you should try being one person for a while."

"Maybe you should see if you have the balls to be someone else, to look like a fool just to learn something. How could you study all those writers—Faulkner, Joyce, Proust, Woolf—and not see they were trying to put a broken world back together? They had no choice. It wasn't just a bunch of fuckin' ideas. They were in pain."

The space beneath my ribs felt tight and hollow. He'd gotten tripped up in the surface of things, in emotions—hackneyed stories beneath which were the real subjects. Maybe I should have talked to him about this years before and helped him channel his vitality in one direction. I thought of Nathalie's inbox, whether by reading it I would understand what she'd seen—him searching and grieving, or afraid, far away in a culture broken by invasion, a place of indecipherable rites and devastated desert landscapes.

I glanced away. People strolled here or there, prim figures like cutouts in the evening. Where was Nathalie now? If I read the emails he sent her, I might see her differently—a muse adored. In his eyes, she might share his urgency for reinvention, his determination to overcome fear, even if doing so required giving up everything they loved.

Faint waves pulsed against the seawall. I thought to speak, to ask the perfect question, the one whose answer would lead to a confession. But what difference would it make now, his guilt or my further humiliation? Maybe I should just accuse—*You, my own brother* . . . But I didn't feel that I had the right.

Neither of us spoke, standing next to each other, facing the harbor, until he sighed.

"Don't you wish we could just stay like this," he said, so softly I had to tilt my head.

Then he walked off and left me there, as if he hadn't been speaking to me at all.

# The Boy and the Lioness

———•◦•———

The young man had an air of desperation, hunched alone at a dining hall table while the other conferees ate and socialized. Francis had been watching him since that morning when he'd overheard him give his name, Amir, to a young woman asking what university he was from and where he grew up. "Here," he'd said, and then "Iraq," appearing flustered, and walked away. At each panel, he sat in the back, clutching a bundle of papers and books as he watched the speaker. The day-long conference was relatively small—a few dozen undergrads, grad students, and professors—and the subject was the destruction of ancient Mesopotamian archaeological sites during the war. In Columbia's classrooms, dimmed for the projection of images, there was a sense of secrecy and import, as if, somewhere in the Pentagon, the nation's best minds were also intent on deciphering symbols and scratches on clay.

"Are you an art major?" Francis asked, nearing a table in the dining hall where Amir sat alone during a break. The others were networking or topping off their coffees.

"Pardon?" he said, glancing up. He lay his arm over photocopied illustrations of Sumerian coins and cylinder seals.

Francis had taken Amir to also be an undergrad but suddenly wondered if he was older.

"What's your area of interest?" he asked.

"I have international interests . . . cultural and historic interests, I mean."

It was clear that he had no interest in talking. He was distracted, dismissive even, as he'd been with the young woman that morning. Francis reached for one of the photocopies.

"I held a cylinder seal once," he said. "From Uruk, in southern Iraq. It was at least five thousand years old. Brilliant inventions and a trademark piece of the era. Are you familiar with their uses?"

Amir's mouth hung slightly open, the flush returning to his skin, and he glanced at the papers. "I'm just learning. It's something of a hobby for me."

Francis didn't wait for him to finish. He explained how the cylinders were rolled over the surface of soft clay, leaving a continuous string of images indicating ownership or authority and preventing anyone from tampering with sealed vessels or doors.

"This image is of the priest-king, which is the best we can do in our terms to describe his role . . ."

Francis's impulse to display his knowledge had always been strong, though he told himself that his desire was to elevate art and history. He went on talking, linking events and dates. He shuffled through Amir's papers as if they were his own.

"You're from Iraq?"

"Baghdad, but my family is in the north now, in Kurdistan."

"So you're Kurdish?"

"No, my father had to leave Baghdad. I'm Arab. Sunni Arab."

Amir was looking at Francis differently, more intently.

"Tonight, after the conference, can I invite you to dinner? You seem to know a great deal about my country's heritage, and I would be interested in hearing more. We can dine with my sister. She's in the city as well."

Francis agreed, thinking, *So I guess he wants me to meet his sister.*

That evening, he took the subway from Columbia to a Greenwich

Village bistro, where Amir again encouraged him to speak of art. Francis's exposition was for Rana now, her hair black like Amir's, her pale-olive complexion in sharp contrast to her lashes and eyes. She was a sophomore at Columbia and Amir was a junior. But though Francis was just months from graduation at Yale, and though he could hold forth for hours on almost any art-related subject, he felt younger than both of them. Amir ordered expensive wine with authority. His blush and air of desperation had vanished. He suggested dishes. He and his sister had poise. She asked Francis what had made him interested in Sumerian art as Amir picked up the bill, laying his fingertips on Francis's wrist to keep him from taking it. As Francis held forth on the mystery of that artistic tradition—its unanswered questions—he felt relieved and chagrined. The meal was beyond his budget.

"We must stay friends," Amir said as they stood outside. He shook Francis's hand, putting his other palm on Francis's shoulder. Though Rana had done little more than provide an audience during dinner, both she and Amir gave him their email addresses and cell phone numbers. No one, not even his professors, had shown such interest in Francis. On the late train to New Haven, he found a seat alone and closed his eyes, trying to understand what had just happened.

———

Shortly after Francis had begun university, his parents divorced. His mother told him that a few years back she'd asked his father to see a therapist and that he'd agreed. Each week he described long, emotional sessions, but three months into his therapy, he said, *Goddamn it*, and confessed that he couldn't do it anymore. He'd been making up the sessions and hadn't been seeing a therapist at all.

"He's a compulsive liar," she told Francis. "He was going to the bar. And the worst part is that everything he described was totally believable."

Francis had been impressed, but she warned him.

"Be careful, Francis; you have him in your genes."

Though his father said he worked for USAID, Francis had once come across his father's journal, its key, and even a manuscript, a screenplay entitled *The Gray Man*, about an aging CIA agent traveling back to Iraq, where he had worked.

Reading it, Francis had no real sense of the main character, who seemed uncertain of who he was himself. Francis wondered if his father had really been in the CIA all these years, but he doubted it. He'd long ago pegged him as a coward, neither able to stand up to his mother nor capable of discussing anything meaningful. He had no recollection of warmth between his parents, or between himself and them.

Whereas his mother was strict and demanding, any attempt at a heart-to-heart with his father quickly devolved into a discussion of current events, during which his father related demographic and GDP statistics of foreign countries, naming major cities and their industries, the areas' cash crops and mineral resources. After finishing a dual degree in Spanish and French, he'd become an Army linguist and later learned Arabic. Francis was pretty sure that if he was ever in the CIA, his job was translating foreign newspapers, since that was pretty much what he did every morning over breakfast.

Even in his journal his father was reticent, the entries undated. Most of them referred to Iraq, sometime in the 1970s. The occasional entry was actually poetic, a quality that Francis attributed less to his father than to the country itself.

*On the roadside, broken glass refracted the sun, a sedan with all four doors burst open, flipped onto its roof like a trodden insect.*

*Women wringing clothes in a gully beneath a broken pipe.*

*Riding behind a marching outfit, a man seated backwards on a mule, like a figure in a Roman fresco, his gun pointed to the hills.*

Further on, he'd made a note to himself: *Change* The Gray Man *to* The Lost Child.

After reading this, Francis studied the journal as he might a poem in a literature class. It often referred to her. This "she" was a woman in Iraqi Kurdistan.

*The Kurds brought her to cook and clean for us. She knew only a few words of Arabic and was from a mountain village where she'd lost her family. When not cleaning or cooking, she stayed in her small room, embroidering pieces of cloth with suns and stars. Once, she sewed a rip in the sleeve of my shirt and returned it with patterns on the shoulders, like something worn by a cowboy.*

The journals later referred to a son or daughter whom his own father had never met, who had been born after he left the country. Francis had been an only child, and the thought of a sibling halfway across the world obsessed him, though he found no means of expressing this other than through his studies of the region's rich artistic past.

Secretly, he entertained the notion that he might find a way to trace his missing sibling, to unite the family through the courage and perseverance that his father lacked.

———

Two weeks after their meeting in Manhattan, Amir and Rana visited Francis in New Haven, again taking him to dinner. Halfway through the meal, Amir changed the subject from Francis's recently completed thesis.

"I have something to confess. I know very little about art. In fact, I'm an economics major. I was at the conference because I was hoping to learn about Iraq's art so that I could help my father."

"Your father works with art?"

"Not really. During the war, my grandfather died. Among his possessions was a small collection that we suspect is quite valuable.

Unfortunately, due to my father's role in helping the US military, he had to leave Baghdad. The family's fortunes have suffered a great deal. It's a long story, but things did not work out as he planned. Now, he is a guest of the Kurds, who have no great love for Arabs."

Amir's voice softened. He lowered his eyes.

"So you see, we hope to sell my grandfather's collection in order to support the family until we can reestablish ourselves."

"I see," Francis said.

"You do?" Amir asked. Rana was watching.

"I think so."

"It is a difficult business," Amir pressed on. "It's easy to get cheated. There are many fake goods on the market, and the dealers are basically thieves. But I told my father about your expertise. He has offered to bring you to Kurdistan for a month after you graduate."

Francis was speechless. He'd made no plans for the summer. Many of his peers had already bought tickets to travel to other countries or received them as graduation presents. With the debt he'd taken on for university, he couldn't permit himself such a luxury.

"It's not dangerous," Amir said. "We would go through Istanbul. In fact, we can spend a few days there. You have seen the Hagia Sophia and the Blue Mosque, right?"

"In books," Francis said, blushing. "You're sure it would be safe for me?"

"Kurdistan? It's safer than Manhattan and certainly safer than New Haven. The security forces, the Peshmerga—their name means 'those who face death'—they care about nothing but protecting their territory."

With Amir, there was no *think about it and get back to me*. They drank their wine. Rana sat, awaiting Francis's decision, smiling when he looked her way. He was attracted to her but sensed a barrier of formality, her questions always measured and polite. When he asked about her life, she never shared anything about herself aside from her studies. He wished he could be alone with her—speak to her, find out what she thought. She excused herself and went to the restroom.

"You could change everything for us," Amir told him, his warm palm on Francis's wrist. "You could save us."

Francis nodded, staring at his plate. Rana returned and replaced the napkin on her lap. He looked at her and then at Amir.

"Of course," he said. "I would love to go."

---

The morning after graduation, after Francis's mother had gone home, his father invited him to breakfast at a nearby diner and showed up smelling of bourbon. He talked of the upcoming election, dismissing Obama and emphasizing McCain's military credentials. He explained polls and constituencies, not eating much, occasionally pausing to prod his scrambled eggs. Afterward, they walked back to campus.

"Dad, you were CIA, weren't you?" Francis asked.

His father stared off, appearing unconcerned.

"What do you want? A good story? Of course I was CIA. You've been digging through my stuff for years. I didn't think I needed to tell you. I mean, for Christ's sake, you were reading my journal."

"It was pretty vague."

"Yeah, well, sorry about that."

They plodded across the green, its turf spongy, not yet firmed up by the summer's heat.

"Here's my favorite story. It's my best. I'll tell it, but you won't believe it. I was in Vallegrande in the fall of 1967."

He said this as if nothing could be more meaningful.

"One morning, the guy I worked under woke me up. He told me to get dressed and to give him the money I had in my pocket. A couple hundred pesos, I guess. He kept telling me to hurry. He said, 'Let's get a look at stone-cold dead history.' At the hospital, he paid a guard to take us to the basement. There was a man lying on a metal table. He had scraggly hair and a beard and was wearing only some ragged pants. He had bullet holes in his arms and chest and in his throat, and his hands were missing. They'd been cut off, very neatly, here, at the wrists."

He turned to Francis. "Guess who it was?"

"Who?"

"Goddamn it, Che! Fucking Che Guevara. He wasn't someone whose case I was working on, but seeing him made me feel that what I was doing was real—that I was part of a larger project. This screenwriting book I read said that every scene has to convey a feeling. That was the feeling in that scene. I mattered. I was a big shot."

Francis and his father stopped walking. The sky was cloud-less, sunlight slanting against their faces as they squinted past each other.

This wasn't the story Francis wanted, not what had captivated him in the journals.

*She had a moon face and small lips, her hair thick about her shoulders. I went to her room and knocked softly. She pulled back the door, holding a skirt on which she had embroidered continuous shapes like the stars in tile work. I gave her a pair of torn pants and she inspected them, and then looked up quickly, at my face, and nodded. When I started to turn away, she touched my wrist. She did it quickly and softly, with just one finger, as if testing the temperature of metal.*

"You know," his father said, "when I was in college, I used to think I was an artistic type. But I wasn't. I spent more years in the field than Che, but he wrote books and made something of his experiences. He left his legacy. I couldn't. The CIA didn't do things openly. That's how it was."

He sighed and cleared his throat—a grating, disappointed sound.

"Dad," Francis said, his heart beating fast. "I want to know about Iraq."

"You know everything there is to know."

"What about the woman and . . . and the child?"

He'd wanted to say, *Your child.*

His father was staring off, his skin drab and slack against the unremarkable bones of his face.

"There was nothing to be done. It was a hopeless situation and it got even more hopeless after I left."

"What about now?"

"Forget it."

They walked until they came to the dorm. Francis turned but his father didn't look at him. He just stood, staring at the building as if counting its bricks.

"What did you think of my screenplay?" he asked.

"What?"

"My screenplay. The one you dug up in my drawer."

"It was okay."

"Yeah, right. I should have put Che in it. I almost did. I was going to have the main character see Che's ghost. But then I thought to myself, why would Che give a fuck about this guy? He's a loser. He's totally irrelevant."

———

Francis lied to his parents and said that he was going with friends to a summer house in Maine, on a lake in the mountains where there was no cell phone reception. In the week before his flight, he scanned hundreds of pages of reference material into his laptop. He read every book and online article he could find about Iraqi art. The frequent mention of its theft made him wonder about the art held by Amir's family. During the American invasion, soldiers had guarded the Ministry of Oil, not the museums and archaeological sites. Thousands of pieces had been looted. Men with bulldozers and AK-47s had dug up ancient cities and hauled off their contents in dump trucks. Cylinder seals were among the most common items to have been stolen since they were difficult to trace, and collectors around the world would pay tens of thousands of dollars for them. Francis sat in front of his laptop, recalling Amir's worried expression during the conference and how he'd kept his distance from everyone.

As promised, Amir, Rana, and Francis spent four days exploring Istanbul. They stayed in a hotel in Sultanahmet, and though Amir hired a guide, Francis found himself adding to the man's explanations, deciphering symbols and elaborating on traditions, glancing at Rana as he spoke.

She rarely addressed Francis, studying him silently when he talked. He tried to make sense of her. She carried herself differently from other young women he knew, dressing in the casual, high fashion of an adult. She clasped her hands in front of her when standing still, listening. He had a habit of affecting a mature way of speaking, and he found himself doing this even more, trying to match Amir's carriage, his refined and bookish accent.

Back in Atatürk Airport, Amir led them to a kiosk on the second floor. It was empty and dark, though a door in the back stood slightly ajar, and beyond it shone a light. He knocked loudly on the counter, and a heavyset man with pouched eyes made his way out. From his jacket, Amir took a wad of American twenties as big as his fist. He bought three tickets.

Francis's stomach began to churn. At the gate, Kurdish men wheeled stacks of bulging suitcases, their well-groomed mustaches a reminder that the look associated with Saddam Hussein was nothing more than the masculine fashion of the region. Beyond the windows, there was the movement of baggage carriers and refueling trucks, a distant liftoff on a dark runway.

They found their seats, three deep on either side of the aisle, Francis at the window. The plane taxied out and stopped. It fired its engines. The brakes released, and runway lights flashed past the wings and dropped away. Briefly, he saw the two sides of the lit city, with the Bosporus dividing them and the dark invisibility of the Black Sea beyond, before the airplane charged into clouds.

Francis couldn't look away from the window. Amir sat next to him, between Francis and Rana, and at some point, he patted Francis's arm. Later, he and Rana slept. The night became clear. The mountainous spine of Turkey passed somewhere beneath them, and then there was the steep sudden banking of the plane, the sparse glow of a city surrounded by mountains, and the wheels hitting the ground too hard.

———

"It is an unfortunate situation," Nasser told Francis. He was nothing like Amir or Rana, short and heavyset, bald on top but for a wisp of Charlie Brown hair. "To inherit such valuable objects at a time when everything leaving Iraq is suspect."

The house wasn't terribly big, with a dusty courtyard in which a few stunted shrubs and herbs had been freshly planted. What Nasser lacked in poise, Leilah, his wife, provided. She was tall and quiet, her features elegant, like those of her children.

"And all this," Nasser said, "it's nothing. You should have seen how we lived in Baghdad. It was once called Madinat as-Salam, the city of peace, named after paradise because of its rivers and gardens."

"Francis knows Iraqi history quite well," Amir said.

"I have heard. I have heard. But did you know what talent we had? When the Americans boycotted everything, we couldn't get enough films, so Baghdadis turned cinemas into theater houses. They wrote and put on plays. Everyone was creative. There was an artistic blossoming."

Again, Amir interrupted, urging Francis to share his knowledge, but in truth Francis knew far more about art than history. His passions had always guided his studies, and even when he'd sat down to read accounts of the country's past, he'd found himself going back to Mesopotamian times, to sculptures and engravings.

"Thank you for coming," Leilah said. "You have done us a great service."

"Yes," Nasser told him. "It is so easy to get swindled here. We know we can trust you. Amir has spoken very highly of you. Very, very highly."

After dinner, Francis asked to see the collection. He worried that Nasser expected something unrealistic, as if Francis might contact dealers or find buyers for the pieces. At best, he could try to identify their origins and value.

The storeroom held generations of furniture, tables stacked on top of tables, rugs rolled up between them, hand-carved chests and engraved folding screens, chairs of all sorts.

"Everything," Amir said, "that furnished our home in Baghdad."

At the back was a Masonite chest, its latch hung with a chrome combination lock.

Amir plugged in a lamp and set it on the floor. He crouched and worked the lock until it clicked.

Inside were at least a hundred small bundles of cloth. Amir balanced on the balls of his feet as Francis unwrapped one. It was a cylinder seal. He'd expected it. The quality was superb. A helmeted man drew the string on a bow.

The next three were similar. Then there was a bag of ancient coins, and he sifted through them. He felt relieved. People had been selling such things in Iraq for centuries, and it was entirely reasonable that they would be in a family collection. Besides, these were among the easiest pieces to sell.

"Are you satisfied?" Amir asked.

Francis nodded. At the bottom was a larger object. He felt Amir studying his hands as he unwrapped it. Gold and what might be ivory adorned a wood carving. He had a sense of recognition that he couldn't place. The high relief showed a boy reclining as a lioness bit his throat. Above him were flowers in bas-relief, and below an engraved mesh a few inlaid jewels remained. He wrapped it and closed the trunk.

"You look tired," Amir told him.

"I am. It must be the jet lag. All of a sudden I feel exhausted."

As they were saying goodnight, Francis asked if he could check his email. The house had a wireless router. He sat in the guest room, on the bed draped with blankets.

The piece came up immediately. The search was too easy. He found a link to Interpol. *Chryselephantine (wood overlaid with ivory and gold) lioness killing a Nubian in a meadow of lotus and papyrus. Origin. Nimrud. 720 BC.*

It had been stolen from the National Museum of Iraq a few years before along with thousands of unprocessed coins and cylinder seals that couldn't be traced. Nasser didn't know what he had. *Lioness Attacking a Nubian* was worth millions. But even if they could sell it, the buyer would have to hide it for decades.

Another article said that governments around the world were drawing up a blacklist of institutions and individual scholars who dealt with stolen items, the intent being prosecution. He shut his laptop.

He lay on the bed, in the dark. They had to have found the piece by accident. No professional would think that Francis could help him legitimize this art for sale. If he tried, his career would be over, and he might spend years in prison.

The shadows of clouds striated the mountains above Sulaymaniyah. The city appeared on the verge of becoming modern. Cell towers and satellite dishes reflected the light. Scaffolding climbed the concrete cores of unfinished office buildings.

A taxi dropped Francis and Amir off in the bazaar. Vendors sold underwear, T-shirts, and cell phones. Money changers sat in chairs with tiny, rickety tables before them, stacks of colorful dinars held together by rubber bands. Men in overalls walked shoulder to shoulder, making way for a yellow Toyota truck loaded with engine parts.

"Is there anything you want to buy?" Amir asked. "Souvenirs or gifts?"

Though Francis knew that he had no choice but to explain that the artifacts were stolen, he had to wait. Coming here, he'd imagined that he would have time to search for his missing sibling. If he brought up the theft, he might no longer be welcome.

His father had written of a teahouse in the bazaar, a place where men went to get information. *Kurdish intellectuals gathered, many soon to leave or else returning from exile, from France, Germany, and Sweden, where they had dreamed of revolution.*

Francis described the place to Amir, saying that a friend had told him about it, that it was historic. Amir stopped. He studied him, squinting as if he had yet to see him clearly. But he agreed to help, and the first man he asked showed them the way.

"Apparently everyone knows it," Amir said, his brow still furrowed.

The doorway opened on a low room. Talk and the clack of dominos and checkers reverberated against tile and yellow brick. Round drums hung on the walls, painted with Kurdish heroes. Framed photos showed freedom fighters with rocket launchers and Kalashnikovs. Multiple No Smoking signs were pasted on the walls, behind a fog of smoke.

"These are the people who fought Hussein," Amir murmured. "They are the ones who hate Arabs."

He hesitated as Francis walked to the corner of the room. There, no more than an alcove with a door and single window, was a bookstore, its walls and half of its floor stacked with books—their covers showing hands clutching bars, tied and bleeding wrists, Bill Clinton, and inevitably enough, Che. A man sat at the center of the room next to a laboring photocopier and reams of paper.

"And what now?" Amir asked. He appeared nervous. "What do you want with this place?"

Francis leaned into the bookstore and asked the man if he spoke English.

"My German is better," he said, "but I am okay." He introduced himself as Jamaal and immediately showed them a thick German-Kurdish dictionary that he'd authored.

"I'm looking for someone," Francis told him. "Someone from long ago. Thirty-five years ago." He sensed Amir at his side, slightly behind him, and didn't glance back.

"You are not even that old," Jamaal said. "That was a bad time. Have you been in contact with this person?"

"No. I was thinking that I could find someone here who might help me."

Jamaal stepped out of the bookstore and closed the door. He motioned for them to follow.

"What is this about?" Amir whispered, his voice a loud, distinct hiss. The color had drained from his face.

"I'll explain later," Francis said. He sensed something being set into motion, felt the heat of pride, of knowing he was in a place that others his age couldn't imagine visiting.

Heads lifted from checkerboards as Jamaal gestured to a far table where the men communicated in sign language.

"The deaf table," he told them, "it has been here forty years. There was once a joke. They were the only Kurds who understood *Das Kapital*. A deaf communist taught the book in sign language. He sat there with a very old translation from the Arabic. We knew he changed the subject each time he made a fist and put it to his chin. That meant he was talking about Lenin."

Jamaal laughed, and Francis forced himself to smile. Amir glanced toward the door.

Four of the seven men at the table appeared to be in their late fifties. All of them wore the Kurdish one-piece outfit, almost like coveralls, though the jacket section was often quite fancy and belted with a sort of cummerbund. The waiter had just served them tea. In each hot glass, a thick layer of sugar lay at the bottom, the tea brimming over into the saucer.

As Francis neared the table, Jamaal said that though he himself wasn't deaf, he knew sign language. The aging men began rapidly signing as Jamaal translated the eager introductions in which they told Francis about themselves and their jobs: making aluminum sheeting, baking bread, or delivering newspapers. One no longer worked, and the others laughed, calling him the Pasha.

But only six of the deaf men had joined the conversation. The youngest sat apart, wearing the fanciest coverall, its top reminiscent of John Travolta's jacket in *Saturday Night Fever*.

"That's Falah," Jamaal said and motioned to him. "He has good connections."

Falah acted as if he hadn't noticed, not even glancing over, as if to preserve his dignity.

Francis nodded, waiting for when he could ask his question.

"I am telling them that you are seeking someone from thirty-five years ago," Jamaal explained as he moved his hands.

The group became agitated, signing all at once.

"They want you to know," Jamaal said, "that they were around then. One of them still has weak lungs from chemical gas. Another was tortured with electricity. That little one shot down two helicopters and later lost a finger and thumb in the aluminum factory because he was daydreaming."

Jamaal said all this without enthusiasm, as if he'd heard it too many times. The smallest deaf man extended his mangled hand. The others grabbed at it, pulling him this way and that, each taking his turn showing it to Francis.

Then they grew silent. Finished with their introductions, Jamaal looked to Falah, who nodded. Francis explained that his father had been here in the seventies and had left a woman who was pregnant with his child. The men became grim.

Falah studied him. He lifted his hand to his chest and made a few rapid, dismissive gestures, as if flicking crumbs from the lapel of his Travolta jacket.

"He will need information about your father," Jamaal said.

Francis gave them his father's name and described his appearance. After a pause, Falah replied.

"Come back in a few days," Jamaal translated. "He will see what he can do."

In the street, Amir walked quickly. Francis hurried to keep up, and once they were a good distance from the teahouse, Amir spun and faced him.

"The Kurds will like you," he said. "They like Americans. They even like Bush for killing Hussein. But Arabs must be careful here. We are accepted but not liked. I know Arabs who have been taken by the police and beaten and questioned. As far as the Kurds are concerned, our people slaughtered their families for decades."

He stood, not moving, his dark eyes glistening as if he might cry.

"How could you not have told me about this?" he asked.

"I didn't know how to."

"Friends share such things."

"I'm sorry," Francis told him, feeling no regret, just a sense of courage, that he was here, doing this, that his ideas and actions could come to fruition. "You're right. So there's one other thing I should tell you."

"What? That you have an entire family here maybe?"

"No. Listen. One of the pieces in the trunk. It belongs in the museum."

"What are you saying?"

"It's stolen."

Amir nodded, very slowly. "I am feeling confused," he said. "There is more to you than I knew. Do you have a motive for telling me this too?"

"No. The piece is well known. It's famous."

Amir appeared genuinely surprised. "Then it's a coincidence. It must be a copy."

"There are only two. One is in the British Museum. The other was stolen from the National Museum in Baghdad. Your father can't sell it. He will get arrested."

"You must be mistaken."

"Amir," Francis said. "You have to trust me. This one is identical to the stolen one, down to the pieces of lapis lazuli in it and those that have fallen out. It has a museum accession number on it. I checked this morning. It's on the bottom."

In the narrow street, they faced each other. Workmen passed, watching as if to make sense of their seriousness.

Amir's eyes had gone cold. "I am no longer the judge of whether you can be trusted. I am afraid that you will have to discuss all of this with my father."

———

Nasser sat on the couch. He smoothed his shirt against his belly and ran his thumb along the front, as if checking the buttons.

"Francis," he said, looking up. "Have a seat. Are you thirsty?"

"No, thank you."

"Amir mentioned your concerns. I'm glad you took the time to express them."

"I'm sorry, sir. I really don't think that these pieces can be sold."

"Just a moment." Nasser patted the air with his hand, though he remained slouched. He linked his fingers on top of his belly. He inhaled and reclined his head and stared off as if at a view, though there was only the wall and low ceiling, the single window hung with drapes.

"When I was a boy," he said, "I wanted to write poetry." He glanced at Francis meaningfully, as if to make sure that he was following. "I was an idealist. My father was a professor. But it was my best friend who most influenced me. He was gifted in everything—science, the arts—but nothing quite inspired him enough to devote his life to it. He loved to think about art though. Someone would tell him an idea and he would reflect upon it, but then, after a few months, if it was mentioned again, he would say, 'That was my idea, wasn't it?' And he'd smile. It was a charming smile. I still entertained some literary ambitions then and he even stole one of my ideas—about a young woman who has forsaken Islam and has been rejected by her family. She wants to return to her village just to look upon the faces of her parents and siblings one last time, but she is afraid to be recognized. So she puts on a veil in order to go back. It was an idea I discussed with him over coffee, and months later, when it came up again, he thought it had been his. Then he smiled that smile, and I couldn't help but like him."

"Yes," Francis said, trying to appear interested. "What's he doing now?"

"I'm digressing. Back then, he wasn't a fan of Saddam or even religion, but then the Americans invaded. Everything was burned. The National Library and the National Archive, the libraries at the University of Baghdad, libraries throughout Iraq. He wept. I have never seen a man cry like that. But then he grew silent. He started composing a book that he called *A Field Guide to Americans*. He'd found a very old copy of Peterson's *Field Guide to Birds* in the studio of a friend of ours, a painter, and he used the same format. He made sketches and listed types of clothes and habitats, who was best to kill and how to do it. The book was an underground success. It was photocopied and updated by freedom fighters, and though he disappeared, he became a hero. But me, I would prefer to be on the winning side. That doesn't mean I don't have ideals. I do. But I have two children, and I know history."

"What did you do for the Americans?"

Nasser waved his hand. "Let's just say I have enemies. I have lost a great deal, and the Americans have forgotten me. That's the problem with giants. They forget the little people, so I will never be remembered as a hero." He looked at Francis. "What would you do if you were faced with this? Exile and death and the possibility that your children will not get educations or have stable lives?"

"I don't know."

"I did not steal those objects. It was an accident. Someone I knew asked me to hold the trunk for him, and a week later he got blown up. So I kept waiting, and then I moved here, and I realized that nobody knows I have these things."

Nasser's eyes, in the dim room, seemed large and heavily veined, calm with conviction.

"I also fought for my country. Maybe I am not as idealistic as I would like to be, but I made a choice to play this dirty game, and when you decide to play a game, you learn the rules and stick to them. That's what I'm doing, and the rules are ugly."

His face lost all warmth and his unremarkable features became harsh.

"Amir and Rana are your friends, so you will help them. Without this source of funding, they will not return to university. They do not know the truth, only that you and no one else can be trusted with such valuable objects. They know how brilliant you are. So here's what you will do for them. You will write a description of each object and explain its value. Then you will put your name and Yale credentials. I know a dealer in Russia, a crooked man, but he is my only hope. For me to negotiate with him, I need your authority. That's how you will help me."

Nasser stared at Francis hard and then shrugged and looked off. He sighed and a hint of controlled anger came into his expression. "So what is this that Amir tells me about your father having been in Iraq? You should not have told anyone that."

———

Crossing Yale's campus at night, Francis had imagined a distant sibling, his own blood mingling in a land where millennia of histories converged, hundreds of ancient holy cities evolving into new ones, the Code of Hammurabi infusing minds, making space for new laws and scriptures, where once Tammuz died each year in fierce summer heat and Ishtar brought water in the spring. For more than twelve thousand years, men and women had lived on these lands, through hot, dry millennia that reduced them, and rainy millennia in which they thrived. Nippur, the temple of the god Enlil, endured for five thousand years.

America felt removed from all that, though he'd begun to see the lineaments of Mesopotamia in his surroundings. Even the stories told in his family, of his great-grandfather and great-great-grandfather fighting in the American Indian Wars, struggling to build cities on the plains, reminded him of the roving armies of the Middle East and Central Asia.

The conquest of North America had created a people with war in their blood, who thought in simple, expansive terms. Francis's father had encouraged him to continue the family tradition of joining the military, though the history was grim: one of his uncles returned from the fields of World War I mentally broken; one died in the Pacific; another had his leg shot off in Korea. His own father had been killed in the Italian Campaign. Francis's father was born in 1942, shortly after the deployment to Europe. But since stories of death and disfigurement weren't persuasive, he most often talked about his grandfather, the Indian fighter who had dominated the family until an aneurism silenced him at 106.

Though Francis's father said that war taught men to understand their primal nature, he showed no sign of this himself—unless the primal truth of men was indifference and passivity. He seemed a hypocrite, the failed offspring of a family of heroes, and his words only increased Francis's interest in art—the result, Francis came to believe, of so many afternoons alone at home with coloring books. And yet, although he was skilled in numerous media, a spark was missing. Francis knew that the art he created was too academic. Nothing he did exuded urgency. At times, he'd imagined that if he took risks this might change. His actions at the teahouse felt like courage, and his only regret was the distrust they had fostered in Amir. Now, the question of the stolen art remained, of whether he could help Amir and Rana. Nasser had told him not to mention the collection to anyone, that the Kurds would sell it themselves and pocket the money. He'd asked him to think of a means of smuggling the objects out of the country. Art theft was as old as humankind. Napoleon stripped the nations he invaded, and the British Empire filled its museums during its expansion, as did the Nazis and Soviets.

An idea came to Francis as he researched the artifacts on his laptop. He could hide them in plaster sculptures of his own.

Nasser became flushed when Francis told him.

"It is a good idea. I can see you are trying to be a friend to my children and to this family. But your chatter at the teahouse"—he said, anger again taking shape from his soft face, tendons rising along his throat—"has gotten around. A Kurdish general has invited us to dinner. He wants to meet you, and we can't refuse. We are their guests after all."

He hesitated, as if to say more. Instead, he called the driver in and told him to go buy plaster. Then he shuffled back to the dark room where he watched television all day.

"So I hear that your father was in Kurdistan," the general said.

Though in his late fifties, he looked strong. A large man, he held his arms against the table as if tensed for action. He had a broad, flat nose and eyebrows half as thick as blackboard erasers. His cropped, gray hair showed the squarish lines of his skull.

All through the meal, Rana and Leilah appeared pale. Amir and Nasser remained silent while the general asked Francis about his father and the missing child.

"What was he doing in Kurdistan? Do you know?"

"He worked for the government. To be honest, he never really talked about it."

"And his name? Your family name?"

"Sheridan. I'm Francis Sheridan. He was William Sheridan."

"Ah. I see. I thought I might recognize it, but you know that government men often change their names. He was here when? In the seventies?"

"I guess."

"I would remember him. I knew them all. My father was also a general."

The conversation eventually shifted to politics and Bush's waning popularity among the Kurds. After dinner, the general gave them a tour of his newly built villa that stood in the hills above the city. It had a terrace and a peanut-shaped swimming pool, but the loose soil around the house was etched with deep lines and gullies where rain and wind had carried it away.

On the drive back into Sulaymaniyah, no one spoke. Rana was next to Francis, and he sensed that she wanted to draw close, to lay her hand on his arm to protect him—but maybe he was imagining this, simply wanting it to be true. He wished that he could talk to her without Amir or Nasser around, or that he'd met her at university as a fellow student, but ever since they'd arrived in Iraq, she'd been even more distant and no longer asked even her few polite questions.

"You don't get it, do you?" Nasser finally said. "I can tell from your face that you don't see the problem."

From his voice, Francis realized how angry he'd been all along. He needed Francis's help but could no longer contain his frustration.

"Kurdistan is not so big. That man knows everyone. He has been fighting Saddam since before you were born. He will have known your father."

"What's wrong with that?"

"Are you *majnun*? Crazy? If your father was here in the seventies, he wasn't doing anything good. The Americans betrayed the Kurds. They set them against Saddam and sold them out right before a battle. The Kurds were massacred. People here have long memories."

Francis had read references to the event but hadn't considered that his father could be capable of such things. He'd taken the words in the journal for the usual political rambling. *The goal wasn't to defeat Iraq—above all, not to push it into the Soviet Union's lap. It was to punish Saddam for working with the Soviets, to maintain equilibrium in the Persian Gulf through destabilization, as if a war of attrition would lead to harmony.*

They rode in silence a while longer, the headlights cutting a swath through the empty landscape.

"Maybe," Nasser said, "maybe no art was made about that battle, so that is why you do not remember."

Francis struggled with the idea of smuggling the masterpiece out of the country even as so many people were struggling to recover others: the Mask of Warka and an Assyrian wheeled firebox of bronze. The Akkadian Bassetki statue, of a boy cast in copper, had been found in a Baghdad cesspool. Many artifacts had no doubt come into people's possession by accident.

Morning sunlight shone in the window as Francis studied the sculpture.

The motif had been common in Babylon. Kings hunted lions, and the animal became the measure of royal power, of godliness. The beast that threatened civilization became the symbol of man's triumph.

But the title most commonly given to the piece—*Lioness Attacking a Nubian*—was wrong. The lioness was not attacking. The Nubian was reclining, wearing shorts and ornamental bands on his arm and wrists. He leaned his head back, exposing his throat as the lioness stood above. One of her legs held his shoulders, her paw on his arm. She bit his throat as if nuzzling, as if she were a lover, and the Nubian's face was calm and surrendered. The markings on her forehead indicated a crown, with a small hole in the center for the missing jewel.

In ancient Nubia, the war goddess Sekhmet was a lioness. Her son, Maahes—god of war, weather, and lotuses, and the devourer of captives—had temples in Taremu, Per-Bast, and Leontopolis, the City of Lions. This was the willful sacrifice of human life, of youth and innocence, to ancient power, to war, and the divine force of nature—a blissful union with our warlike nature.

Carefully, Francis placed the sculpture in a small wooden box that he covered with plaster. Amir and Rana had trusted him, and if he had betrayed their trust, this might set things right. He worked fast, sensing that he didn't have much time. When he'd returned from the general's house, he'd had the impression that the objects on his desk had been moved—his laptop or the papers near it. In the house, no one spoke, the heat of the day gathering like expectation in the dim rooms.

He molded the plaster around the box into a bust and then took a kitchen knife and began to carve a face. But each one that came to mind wore an expression of anger or disappointment or fear—Amir, Nasser, and Rana. He considered rendering Che as he'd appeared in Korta's famous photograph, *Guerrillero Heroico*, but as he thought this, he recalled his father's face and was startled by his own disgust. There was nothing heroic about William Sheridan or his past.

Francis's hand began to move, tracing an outline, an impression of a face, maybe his own had he been born in this country. It became that of the reclining boy, the image of the artifact still clear in his mind.

———

Late the next afternoon, soldiers arrived at the house and asked everyone to get into an army jeep.

"It's good to see you again," Falah told Francis. He was at the wheel, his hair flattened as if from sleep, though his Travolta outfit was impeccable.

Francis stared at the fleshy lips that he hadn't thought capable of producing words.

Falah laughed. "Deaf men hear things others don't. I appreciate what they know. My father was deaf."

The wide boulevard cut through the city, segmented with rotaries, and at the center of each stood an officer, directing traffic with animated authority, or slouched, arms crossed, letting cars rocket past.

At the station, the general and an American army officer in desert fatigues sat at a table. Falah motioned Francis and the family toward chairs, and a moment later soldiers brought in the trunk as well as the plaster bust.

The general stared at the wall, the skin of his neck dark, his deep-set eyes fixed.

"So you're Francis?" the officer said. His name tag read *Estrada*, and his accent was faintly Southern. "Have a seat."

He asked a few questions about why Francis had come to Kurdistan and then said, "What can you tell me about the contents of this trunk?"

Francis shrugged. "It's the family collection. It belonged to their grandfather, and they asked me to help identify the pieces."

"Really?" The soldier had pale blue eyes, the whites faintly bloodshot. His build was muscular, and stubble shadowed his wide jaw.

"Yes, really."

He turned a computer screen toward them and opened a folder that Francis had created on his laptop. It must have been hacked and copied when he was at the general's villa. There were the images of cylinder seals and of *Lioness Attacking a Nubian*.

"You recognize these?"

"Of course. I majored in art history at Yale. My thesis was on Mesopotamian art."

The officer opened his eyes a little wider. He glanced at the screen and then at the general, who still hadn't looked at them but who shrugged.

"This stuff is stolen," the officer said. "I don't know about the plaster bust, but the cylinder seals and the coins were taken from a museum."

Francis glanced around and met Rana's gaunt stare. He measured his own intentions. He could admit to the truth and go home.

"This is absurd," he told the officer.

"Pardon me?"

"Those seals and coins, there are thousands like them in Iraq. If they were from the museum, they would have accession numbers."

"They weren't registered yet."

"And that's grounds for accusation? You need proof that these were stolen, and there isn't any. Their grandfather bought them. I agree that they're cultural treasures. That's what they wanted me to determine. But this is a private collection. It was legally purchased. If the pieces go to the museum, the family should be remunerated."

The officer sighed and nodded once, slowly.

"Nothing here has an accession number," Francis said, entirely uncertain as to the legalities in this situation. "Nothing," he repeated.

The officer looked around the room. "Would you all mind if I speak to Francis alone?"

The general stood and motioned to Falah and then glanced toward Francis, not quite at him. "Falah will take the others home. I will drive you myself when we're finished."

As the others left, the officer motioned Francis into an office and extended his hand.

"I'm Hugh," he said.

"Francis."

"Hey, sorry about all of this. I see your point. This isn't my usual job. I got the call to act as an intermediary. I guess I was the closest." He rubbed his chin. "And hell, I haven't even recovered from last night. These boys up here know how to drink."

Francis didn't smile. Hugh sounded less authoritarian, more unsure of himself.

"So listen. I want to make sure you weren't speaking under pressure."

"I wasn't."

"I'm going to give you my cell number. If anything happens or you realize that maybe the family has been lying to you, call me and I'll make sure you're safe. You're a US citizen, and we do our best to take care of our own here."

This was the moment to tell the truth, Francis knew, to be escorted out and sent home. He would never speak to Amir and

Rana again, but it hardly mattered. He barely knew them, had shared little with Amir and had exchanged no more than a few perfunctory words with Rana. And yet, if he told the soldier the truth, all of this would be over for him but not for them, who had done nothing wrong.

Hugh slid a note card across the desk. His number was on it. He was staring at Francis differently now, as if he'd read or recognized something in his expression, though Hugh's gaze was open, almost boyish—less that of a man sensing a lie or perceiving guilt than that of one who has recognized a familiar face.

"You can call me," Hugh finally said. "In the meantime, we'll check things out. If the story's true, we'll return everything to the family or negotiate something. To be honest, I don't really know. I probably won't be in charge. So good luck."

"Thanks," Francis said, afraid for the conversation to end and yet sounding more dismissive than he'd intended.

—————

Sparrows traversed the cooling sky, as if coasting on shadow. The mountains darkened, the pale lines of roads standing out. A single light glittered like a rising star near the radio tower.

The general sped through the city. It wasn't the way to Amir's house.

"That was good lying," he finally said.

"It wasn't lying."

"I can tell a liar. But what does it matter? It's not what I care about."

They were leaving the city. They'd come upon a military checkpoint, had been waved through, and were riding now between brown, eroded fields.

"Where are we going?"

"I want you to look at something."

"What?"

"A grave. I want to get your opinion."

"Isn't it late?"

"No," the general said and then asked about Francis's father, more directly than he had during the dinner. He spoke as if trying to sound casual, but his voice remained tense. He wanted to know who the woman was, the mother of the lost child, and Francis explained what little he recalled from reading his father's journal: the young woman who'd been brought to cook for the agents, the intimacy between her and his father, the pregnancy, and his father's flight.

*I had to be out of the country within the hour. She was at the bazaar, buying food. I took two thousand American dollars in the smallest currency I could find—money intended for prospecting for intelligence. I left it inside her bag of embroidered cloth.*

"Do you think," Francis asked, "that the child can be found?"

"No. Your father could have told you that. He was a knowledgeable man. He would have known what was coming."

The Zagros Mountains appeared, familiar from Francis's readings: the border with Iran, treeless and ragged, dun-colored in the darkening haze of distance.

The general veered from the road onto a barely visible path that ran behind an earthen mound the size of a house. He stopped the truck, got out, and took a shovel from the back. Francis followed him, and the general pushed the shovel into his hands.

"I want you to tell me when this grave was dug."

"What grave?"

He pointed to the foot of the mound, and Francis wondered if it was an archaeological remain of some sort.

"The one right here," the general told him. "Dig. You will see it."

"I don't see anything."

"Start digging."

Above the mountains, the sky was extinguished, and far to the west the sun dissolved into a mist of crimson light.

The ground was soft. With each swing, Francis sank the shovel blade deeper, and a hole quickly opened up at his feet. He wasn't used to this sort of work. Almost immediately, blisters formed on his palms. Soon, it was completely dark.

"I don't see a grave," he said, sweating hard.

"Keep digging," the general told him, his voice harsh now.

Francis dug until his hands were swollen and raw. The shovel handle was wet, with blood or sweat; it was too dark to see.

"I have to stop," he panted, the hole now waist deep. He was afraid and couldn't catch his breath. His hair clung to his forehead. Sweat dripped into his eyes.

The general had been standing near the truck, and he took something from beneath the seat and came over and stood above Francis. He aimed a pistol at Francis's head.

"Keep digging."

Francis's arms and legs shook. His fingers cramped against the wood, but he no longer felt them. He told himself not to cry—that he would survive this. He dug, and only when he stood shoulder deep did he stop.

"I can't see anything," he said. "There's no grave. I can't help you."

"Yes, you can." The general's voice had changed, thick as if with emotion or grief. It did not sound like rage. "Tell me how old this grave is or I will shoot you."

The black sky revolved as Francis swayed weightlessly, staring up. The muzzle of the gun was faintly darker than the night.

"I'm sorry. I didn't know," Francis said, forcing himself not to cry. "Amir and Rana didn't know. Only Nasser knew. They're both innocent."

"Yes, innocent," the general repeated. "You Americans and your innocence. But you are not innocent, are you?"

"I didn't want to get them in trouble."

"So kind of you. So generous. But I don't care about that."

"Then what do you want?"

"I don't want anything. We are here because of your father."

"I don't understand." But gradually Francis did.

"He was stationed here. That's why I had your computer searched. For photos. I recognized him. His name wasn't William when I knew him. For three years, he was our friend. We did everything he asked. We could have defeated Saddam."

"But that doesn't involve me. Whatever happened isn't my fault."

"This isn't about you. It's about killing your father's son."

"Why?" Terror and regret gripped the muscles of Francis's throat, but he commanded himself to think, to stay calm. Time unspooled, stars pulled free of their fabric, and briefly he could not find himself, didn't know who or where he was.

"Why?" the general repeated. "You're educated. From what I recall of your literature, vengeance can be taken on the son for the father's crimes." He spoke as if to sound reasonable, but his voice trembled. He calmed himself, strangely also gasping, as if he too were terrified. "I had a few years of education in England. Revenge was a popular subject in the books I had to read. So was sons walking the paths of their fathers, because it is our nature to return to the places that create us."

"This isn't my place."

"That's hard to say. You are here. You have returned."

"I didn't return because I was never here before."

"Yes, another forgotten notion. But the son of a king, is he not also the king? We return to the places of our fathers even if we have never been there ourselves."

No moon had risen to light the general's face. His silhouette hung against the sky.

"What did he do?" Francis asked. Every part of his body shook uncontrollably.

"One day," the general told him, "one day we had Saddam's army pinned down and the next the Iranians and Americans were gone, and Saddam knew before we did. We were slaughtered. Thousands killed. Hundreds of thousands forced out of the country, into Iran and Turkey. Hundreds of thousands relocated to the south by Saddam. We were massacred. Your father came here drunk on self-importance. He used us and threw us away. So if you want to know where your brother or sister is, lie down in this dirt."

Francis could barely stand. He had to be calm, to think of a way out.

The general no longer spoke with rage, but in a whisper that terrified Francis with its intimacy.

"I lost my brother that day. He was also your father's friend."

On the road, the sound of a large engine drew close. Headlights fanned out, and at the curve beyond the mound, a truck down-shifted, the low gear thrumming in the empty night. The general looked up and waited. His features were swollen. Light shone on his eyes and teeth and on his wet face, his pocked and fissured skin. Then the truck passed beyond the mound and was gone.

Briefly, Francis thought that if he kept the conversation going, he might be saved. But he was wrong. All that he wanted was as unreal as a daydream, and he gave up this desperate longing to be far away. As he calmed, he sensed the distant shuttling of thoughts he hadn't been aware of, the swift passage between intuition and reason, and then his mind quieted, and he saw his place. He saw himself and the general, gazing at each other in the dark, the raw earth spreading out around them. Francis studied this moment as if holding it in his hands, as if he might trace the relief of a boy and a soldier carved upon the night.

"Tell me when this grave was dug," the general commanded.

But Francis had surrendered his terror. He'd accepted this moment as if it had been shaped centuries ago. He looked up at the general.

"He betrayed me too."

"What?"

"He betrayed all of us. He was a coward. He was a nobody. I've hated him all my life."

The general lowered the gun. He rubbed his thick jaw and his neck and leaned his head back and sighed. He stood like that for a long time, breathing loudly in the dark.

"If you need to kill me," Francis told him, "I understand why. I don't want to die, but I understand your reasons. Except that I don't even know if he'd care."

The general stood, staring at the night. Francis wondered how much longer he could hold this moment, this feeling of acceptance that might be the wisdom of desperation or his mind's final ruse, or simply adrenaline and the brain's chemicals cutting away his connection to the body so that he could die in peace.

"If you can recognize a liar," he said, "then you know I'm not lying."

The general slowly looked down at him.

"Come," he said. "Get out."

He motioned Francis to the truck.

Later, as the lights of Sulaymaniyah lifted into view, Francis felt his chest release, felt the longing and confusion of his body rush back.

"The grave," he asked, gasping, "when was it dug?"

"That grave," the general said without inflection, "it was dug today, but it turns out that it's not a grave after all."

———

They sat in the station. The general poured them each a paper cup of whiskey, and they drank beneath the flickering fluorescent bulbs.

"There's a piece that I hid," Francis told him. "It should be returned to Baghdad."

The general got up and opened the locker where the artifacts had been stored, but the plaster bust was missing, nothing else. He said something in Kurdish with a muted intensity that suggested profanity.

"Someone must have taken it," he said and sat heavily. He ran his palm over his cropped, gray hair. "What was in it?"

Francis explained, and little by little, as if to fill the silence that the general allowed, he described the artifact inside, its history and symbols. He described the reclining figure and the powerful creature poised above, holding him.

The general listened, his head lowered, eyes nearly hidden beneath his brows. Something had passed. Rage and grief had burned through them and left them exhausted. The present, even in this drab room, glittered.

"Forget about the woman and her child," he said. "They are dead, or in Iran."

Francis nodded. He closed his eyes and sighed, feeling the tender motion of his breath.

"There is a flight in the morning," the general told him. "To Istanbul. You will be able to find your way home from there."

Francis opened his eyes. "What about Amir and Rana?"

"I am not here to punish."

"And the sculpture? What about it?"

The general shrugged.

"Sooner or later, everything comes home."

# II

(1879–1945)
CANADA
SOUTH AFRICA
ENGLAND
THE UNITED STATES
FRANCE

# A Song from Faraway

W hen Joseph was five, his mother placed the fiddle on the kitchen table, its dark varnish nicked and rubbed to wood in places. Beyond the open door, gulls called and flashed over the ocean, the wind rising and pulsing.

"I cannot hope," she said, "that you'll be as brave or as good a man as my brother, Louis, but I can ask that you be half as good a fiddler as he was."

Already in Joseph's ears, as if inside waves and wind, was the sound not of his dead uncle's fiddle, which he'd never heard, but of his less brave and less good father's—the exuberant rhythms played on the docks, in the dance hall, or even on the stoop of the house, in the evening, when there was no fun to be had elsewhere and nothing else worth doing.

Its music would follow Joseph through provinces and countries, through lives so different that, if his various selves met at a crossroads, they'd be wary strangers and refuse to shake hands.

He would carry the fiddle over three continents and through two wars.

"All the Empire's people have been scattered out across the world," his mother told him as if she had pity for the Scots and Irish. But she had none. She told her stories, of her Acadian ancestors that the British deported from Nova Scotia in 1755, "Splitting families and dumping them here or there along the coast all the way down to New Orleans."

Moving her finger up the map, she showed Joseph how their ancestors had to climb—"Back up the continent," she said—as if the east coast of the United States were a sea cliff above which sat New Brunswick. They resettled in Caraquet, where she grew up on the southern shore of the Baie des Chaleurs, across from the Gaspé Peninsula. But in January of 1875, eight years after Confederation, the provincial government passed the Common School Act with the intention—"*avec l'intention*," she reiterated—of eliminating not just Catholic values but the French language itself.

"That was when my brother, Louis, your uncle, Louis Mailloux— don't you forget his name—joined the other men to organize riots and show those damned English constables that we were the rightful owners of that place."

Joseph's uncle, Louis, was nineteen when he defended the French language and an Englishman shot him. She told this story so often it seemed he'd been shot time and again, as if his breast could not be pierced enough to shed a quantity of blood worthy of her tears.

But unlike Joseph's mother, his father, whom she'd met the summer he'd gone to Caraquet for work, did not tell stories, which was why Joseph's mother didn't know, until she was pregnant, that his father's last name, Dillon, was not a French variant poorly spelled in a register by a near illiterate colonist but an Irish surname from County Clare.

A handsome sailor, he spoke perfect French and knew little of his history, just that his own father had such a mighty craving for potato he'd fled to Canada to get some, but mostly ate cod, and fell in love with a young woman in Miscouche, Prince Edward Island. Though suckled at her French breast, Joseph's father was to be schooled on his father's fishing boat and fiddle.

At the time of the riots, Joseph's mother was seventeen and pregnant, and as if to distance her from her grief over Louis's death, his father sailed her to his family home on Prince Edward Island, where she learned from his mother the origins of his deceased father. And six years later, like his father, he disappeared on the ocean, either over it or into it, escaping or dying. She was furious regardless, as if he'd fled to death with the passion of a man rushing into another woman's arms.

From that day, she referred to him as *le maudit Irlandais*—the damned Irishman.

————

Joseph suffered. His gut boiled when he thought of his father, that he'd never again walk with him to the docks or be nourished with the rhythms of his fiddle. He calmed only when he played— reels and stomps and jigs—though he sometimes had to pause and gasp, realizing that he'd been holding his breath.

Each evening, he succumbed to his mother's scrubbing, for she washed him daily as if to wring the Irishman from his body. She claimed she should have named him Louis and not let his father dirty him with his own name.

Her stories also tried to wash his father away. As if she had to tell all injustices, she taught him the island's history, how it had been part of Acadie and called l'Île Saint-Jean. The British had forcibly deported the island's French inhabitants as well, back in 1758, and forty years later the King changed its name to that of Prince Edward, one of his whelps.

Through stories, she explained away the existence of Joseph's father. He'd been too handsome to be resisted, skilled at seduction.

She'd been young. She hinted at her own passion before saying, "He was a liar. He never told his truth—the truth of his blood."

But when she was angry, there was one story above all others, the death of his uncle Louis Mailloux in Caraquet and the riot over the school laws that intended to destroy their religion and culture. Her brother, Louis, was meeting with other Acadian leaders in an attic when the English sheriff came into the house and led his men upstairs. One of the Acadians shot a constable. The English opened fire, and Louis was killed.

———

Joseph was no talker, tightlipped, with a pugnacious chin, his jaw wide, muscled and clenched so that no words escaped. He had the dark hair and crystal eyes of an Acadian, but, like his father, he was freckled—a changeling face, he'd been told by a girl he went to school with. As for stories, the only ones he didn't mind were about Louis's fiddling. He liked the idea of music filling homes so that old and young could dance.

To flee his mother's talk and be with men, he worked from a young age and doing so learned English. He roved the coast and listened to Scots, Irish, Acadian, and French musicians. When even they stopped to talk, he felt impatient. People were composed largely of nonsense, their smoking and drinking as useless as their stories and boasting and endless flirtations. He especially hated church and confession—stories of misery and wrongdoing.

Alone, he practiced. He had to hear a tune but once, his ear funneling it into his brain. But the song he preferred was the first his father had taught him, a simple melody his father had played often alone, on the stoop of the house or the hill overlooking the strait. It was like nothing else Joseph had heard on the island—slow, rising and falling away and rising again, like a plea that would never be

granted, though it would be made again and again. It must have
been a song from faraway, and it made his mother angry.

"If you play that damned Irish song," she said, "I'll take your
fiddle."

Though she'd once gone to the town hall to change his surname and been refused, she did not take his fiddle, for such a thing
should be used. She did, however, tell him that his uncle's ghost
would curse him each time he played his father's song.

He played anyway. He walked out along the coast and stood
beneath its bluffs and played to the sea.

———

Silent, he grew into a broad-shouldered man, arms corded from
fishing, hands calloused, their long, thick fingers graceful upon
the fiddle's neck. His freckled mug remained eerie: ice-blue eyes
and coal-black hair, a slight nose and wide, determined jaw.

Evenings, when his tireless love of song infuriated his mother,
he escaped to the docks or tavern to play. Raised without siblings,
he was tough from defending himself against boys from other families. After brawls, he savored his own bruises, though no amount
of ruckus quieted his unrest. As he played to the sea, he saw himself crossing it, on the deck of a ship, far coasts appearing like mist
at the watery line of the horizon. But his mother needed him, so
he stayed.

Into his twenties, he remained solitary. He had but one love
interest, a red-headed Scots girl whom, after he spoke to her on the
road before the house, his mother called *un vaut-rien*. "Her family
has made nothing of itself," she claimed. Joseph didn't approach
the girl again, and after a year she was engaged to another man.

As one endures rain on a long walk, Joseph endured his mother's
stories and found respite in work. Once, at the docks, a recently

married man teased him, asking how his wife was. Joseph stood as
the wind flapped the loose end of a sail and waves sloshed on rocks.
Then he understood. He stepped forward and caught the man's collar and held his head down as if to wash the hair of a struggling
child. He beat the man's face until the others pulled him away.

———

Late that October, the fishermen discussed the British war in
South Africa, against the Boers, a sort of Dutchmen, it seemed,
who refused to let their lands be taken by the Empire. No one
seemed to quite understand the origins of the war or its reasoning.

"It's about gold," a man said.

"Not just gold, but the rights of British citizens working the
gold in Boer lands."

"That's an excuse."

"Everything's an excuse."

Sometimes these arguments turned into fights between an
English and an Acadian youth, tussling over an insult made to the
Empire.

But how the Empire staked its claim, rightful or not, didn't
interest Joseph. In the dark kitchen, after his mother had gone to
sleep, he considered how uncomprehending she would be. And
yet she deserved to be alone. He packed his fiddle and a duffel of
clothes. Surely, he'd be home within the year. He left a note. *Je pars
en voyage*. Nothing more.

Ice had yet to choke the seaways, and from Charlottetown he
found passage to Gaspé, a port of merchants and fishermen con-
gregated on slopes above the windy gulf, and then to Montréal,
working aboard a steamer, swabbing decks as he admired the
rough coasts of the Saint Lawrence.

At the volunteer enlistment office in Montréal, he gave his
name.

"Joseph Dillon."

"Irish?" the man said.

"Yes. From Prince Edward Island."

"Good man. We can use recruits like yourself. The French out there don't have the stomach for war. They're a weaker race, you know."

"I know it," Joseph said, considering he might learn something from war, about courage or strength. He imagined his mother hearing that he'd be fighting as a British subject. Later, in training, he stood among the troops and, as if to justify his choice, joined them in "God Save the Queen," singing wildly.

Evenings, he played his music. He no longer had to listen to stories of the starved, deported, and oppressed dead whose suffering made the present hopeless, as if each day would finish with a few men in an attic being fired on by British constables.

———

The war was going badly. The British had tried to conquer these lands once before, twenty years back, and lost. Again, the Boers, hardy farmers accustomed to the hills, were giving a punishing offensive.

The first days of Joseph's deployment, he marched with the other men—under the sun, over an arid, scarped earth to relieve the embattled British. He thrilled at the shape of the land—the high rolling plains broken by mountains, the sky bright and open and empty. But when he got to the front, his pleasure waned. His first night he helped gather dozens of British dead, shot when rushing a Boer line. The following morning, the battle raged along a river whose water poisoned the dehydrated troops with typhoid. He and his companions dug trenches as the Boers fired in the distance, camouflaged among stones. He sensed the fierce persistence with which men defend their home.

War was confusion. Echoed shots. The senses reaching out, ears listening for each ricochet, eyes following constant movement. Beyond the dusty plain, big, silver-veined rocks glittered. Bullets hit the ground and threw up dust. Their postures distinct with fear, men charged—some birdlike or prancing, others hunched low and jabbing their feet at the earth.

They broke the Boer ranks, running and leaping past their own dead, firing into trenches. On dry grass, retreating enemy soldiers collapsed and flopped about like fish.

That evening, Joseph walked out from camp and stood below a bluff and played. His father's song resonated in the thin wood, and as it rose, beside him, a figure seemed to stand, retreating with slow backward steps from the music: a mirror of his self or of some part of it, or a memory. He closed his eyes and still he sensed it.

An officer scrambled up the hill.

"Shut that damned thing up. What are you doing?"

Joseph lowered the fiddle. As he came into camp, the men sat, staring at him with liquid eyes. Their faces were gaunt, their smudged brows lit with firelight.

———

For more than two years, the war dragged on. With the wealth of their gold mines, the Boers had purchased modern weapons from Germany, and so only with the largest force Britain had ever sent overseas were their cities taken.

Though the British annexed the Transvaal Republic and the Orange Free State, the Boers fled into the hills and fought a withering resistance. Under Lord Kitchener, the British built blockhouses at bridges and along roads to protect the transport of goods. To cut off support for the guerillas, they burned farms. They captured Boer men and deported them throughout the colonies, to Saint Helena, Ceylon, Bermuda, and India.

Joseph hated this work, the policy of scorched earth—hated it most when it was his turn to set fire to a home. Between expeditions, he tried to rest and forget, to inure himself and remain strong against the fevers that felled more men than did bullets. Camps grew full, thousands of women and children, faces shrunken and skeletal, hands gripping wires like the claws of birds.

"How many are there?" he asked an officer.

"The whole damned country as far as I can tell. One hundred thousand blacks maybe. We've sent almost twenty thousand Afrikaners to other colonies, and good riddance. It's the women and children I hate to see. If these people had the good sense of . . ."

War, Joseph understood, had little to do with those who fought it, which was why soldiers had to brag about it, to lay claim to it through stories and make it their personal measure and that of their people.

On expeditions, the land was empty.

———

Crossing the veld toward distant rocky kopjes, an Irish fiddler joked that he wouldn't mind riding under the British standard if he could use it for shade. He explained his own bad luck to be here, where he'd had to make war against fellow Irishmen who'd come to Africa to fight alongside the Boers. He put a name to the song Joseph had learned from his father.

"*An Cuilin*," he called it, and another Irishman agreed. They listened as Joseph played. They asked where he was from, and for him to play again, and in their faces Joseph saw that the song had changed, that it carried traces of a continent foreign to them. At times, in its melody, he heard his mother telling him that Acadians had lived hundreds of years by the sea, where he should have stayed.

Evenings in British-occupied towns, the soldiers who had

fiddles or harmonicas or guitars played together. Joseph went to hear Arab and Jewish musicians in their rough quarters near the markets. Before dawn, he sometimes heard the mellow chanting of Indian workers and merchants at worship. At night, when black prisoners sang, he linked his father's melody to their words.

Over those years, he saw the soldiers with whom he played music shot down or wounded, or made strange from herding families into the crowded, reeking camps.

After battles, Joseph's senses hovered above his body, echoing his movements. Nights, he woke, moonlight piercing his skin. He walked into the dark. His hands trembled until he began to play, and then his senses, which hung in the air, came alive, as if the music rose and caressed the immense ear of the sky.

---

The war ended on May 31st, 1902, and for two years Joseph traveled the ports of Europe, listening to music in concert halls and bars and on street corners—German operas and Romani songs. When his war earnings ran out, he played for money. He had his uncle's violin restringed by an old Jewish man in a shop.

Still, in the night, he woke from images of women and children behind fences, bodies rank with illness, or the black folk in the camps, whose men hadn't fought. He took the fiddle from the case and played softly. The other lodgers never complained though his music seeped through the vents of old hotels and boarding houses. His father's song washed him with longing for his northern sea, for the island's landscape, even though when he had been on that island, the melody had made him dream of countries faraway.

He'd been gone five years when the island appeared against the water. It was summer, and after he docked, he walked all night and into the next day, from Charlottetown to Miscouche.

She was sitting on the porch, wrapped in a shawl, her hair still

black though her face had paled. In her hands, she held the Bible
like a talisman.

"*Maman*," he called.

"You have come back?" she said.

Standing before the porch, he nodded once.

"Where did you go?"

She sat, clenching and unclenching the muscles of her jaw, as if
to forestall grief or rage, the skin of her face slack.

"To war."

"What war?"

He told her. He told her a little of what he'd done, and she
appeared confused.

"It was terrible," he said, "much that I saw. But I saw good
things too."

"You fought for the English?"

"*Oui.*"

She lowered her head.

"Go inside. Make yourself at home."

———

They established a tentative peace. He worked at the docks and
when he returned, she was often in the kitchen, asleep in her chair,
her black hair strewn about her shoulders. Days, she moved slowly,
and, when he pretended not to be watching, haltingly. At times
she coughed. She stopped and hunched a bit, put her fist to her
lips and cleared her throat. But she still told her stories, of the
Acadians' struggle to return home to Caraquet, and of Louis.

When there was work to be had at the docks, he took it, hating
the questions of other men. They discussed the war a bit, asking
his opinion, but he just shrugged, not interested in the stories they
told to make themselves more than fishermen.

On occasion, young women and widows paid him attention,

but he had little interest, his nights haunted and sleepless even though he worked days with compulsion. He'd never wanted—had hardly thought about—a wife or children. What space his music left, memories filled. On the road home, people scurried, fragile in the first bleak November light.

Trying to sleep, he twisted in his blankets. If he hadn't gone, others would have. As if in a woman's embrace, he sweated and clutched the headboard until the wood creaked, though with the few whores he'd known, in Europe and Africa, he'd been uncertain and restrained.

He dressed and walked out and played to the sea, following melodies like paths over the water, though all the while, a figure seemed to stand close, smelling of dust and rank clothes, of exhausted, disheartened flesh.

His dreams were worse in winter, and after two years home the prospect of another season of stories, of sleepless cold, forced him back to sea. He told his mother and she simply nodded, streaks of white now in her hair and her cough persistent.

He signed on a merchant ship that ran the American coast, New Orleans to Baltimore, New York and Boston, up to Halifax and St. John's and Montréal. He stayed with the crew for over three years, the work exhausting him so that he slept without dreams, his days busy, allowing him not to think about his reason on this earth or the heart's obscure design.

In ports, he found that watching strangers had something of the divine in it. The intimate, universal gestures of work purified men, but that changed when they told their stories full of prejudices. On the Halifax wharves, one man, large and black, fought another, clearly winning, until his gut was slashed. The inn stood just beyond where the man lay in his blood as the audience left. But later, from the dormitory, Joseph heard him weeping and made out the word *maman*. Everyone in the dormitory was silent. Eventually he got up and shut the window.

In the spring they put ashore in Rivière-au-Renard, on Québec's Gaspé Peninsula, to repair an engine. Not far from the docks, a family worked, a father with three girls, the eldest perhaps eighteen. As he pulled in nets of herring, they gathered them in buckets. The low sun was golden along their arms, the sea quiet and their voices lost behind the cries of gulls.

Joseph watched as the eldest girl lifted a bucket. She was barefoot, in a dress cut to her knees, and when her dark hair fanned across her shoulder, she paused to twist it into a bun. The father had pulled in another net of herring, and in some places, the girls were up to their calves, the herrings' gills stretching for air.

"You've more work than you can do in an evening," Joseph told them, and it was true. The father, Albert Dubé, welcomed his help, and the girls introduced themselves. As the descending sun shone silver lines on her black hair, the eldest stepped close.

"It's a pleasure to meet you," she said and, lifting her chin, told him her name: Félicité, like a promise, or a warm wish. Her cotton dress was napped from wear, and he kept his gaze to the newly stitched seam at her shoulder.

"*Oui, c'est un plaisir,*" he said.

That night they invited him to the farm for dinner, and Félicité read from Hebrews. She sat sternly, lines on her brow and at the corners of her mouth, but her voice was rich with emphasis and, in places, what sounded like concern.

"These all died in faith not having received the promises, but having seen them afar off, and were persuaded of them, and embraced them, and confessed that they were strangers and pilgrims on the earth. For they that say such things declare plainly that they seek a country . . ."

The next morning, a bright, blustery day, Joseph didn't return to the boat. He asked Albert if there was work to be done on the farm, and he went up beyond fields overlooking the gulf, to the forest's edge. He stood in last year's trampled goldenrod and split seasoned logs for fence posts.

Near noon Félicité climbed the slope with an old coffee can filled with water. He took it in both hands, and as he lifted it, the sky flashed along the ribbed metal. It was nothing like the shadowed water in a ship's barrels, but clean, with perhaps the faintest hint of tin.

"You are so kind—*si gentil*," she said. "S*i bon*."

She plucked a dried goldenrod head and crumbled it, and then scrutinized her fingers and palm, and looked at him again. He wanted to say something about the richness of the land that ran from the sea to the forest, or about seeing her and her sisters on the shore.

He gazed north, to where sea shadowed into horizon. This family, in his mother's eyes, were his people, this province more home than his island. Light slanted against the water, the sun bearing down on the horizon's stone-blue haze.

He almost said no as she took his hand.

———

He rented a room in a boarding house but supped with her family each evening. Many in town had known hardship and uncertainty, had been sailors unable to free themselves from voyage, and they tried to make a place for him, noting that he didn't drink or even smoke, just played music. The curé visited to tell him that the Royal Post needed a mailman.

"It's a simple job, but the responsibility is great. If the mail is stolen or lost, you will be held accountable." He spoke the legal words for being wanted by the authorities: *poursuivre par la reine*— pursued by the Queen.

Each journey lasted five days, to Bonaventure and back, and

Joseph didn't mind, for something in him couldn't stay still. He rode a sorrel loaded with bags and the communion wine for parish churches and came to know where he was on the road by a lone, wind-blasted oak or an old farmstead. He passed Percé, shielded from waves by a rock the size of a castle, and in the rock, a hole so large a fishing sloop could sail through. The scents of silage and cattle and onion fields reached him. There were brilliant *épilobes*, the fireweed that grew along forests and pastures.

Each weekend that summer, when he was in Rivière-au-Renard, he and Albert fished or worked on the farm. He'd worried that he had nothing to offer, but he was a good worker and suddenly, it seemed, a kind man.

As he rode, he considered that Caraquet lay just across the bay from Bonaventure. When he thought of his mother's stories now and of Louis, he imagined the anger of the Boer, their rage repeated, breathed from generation to generation through story.

To keep himself from thinking, he fiddled as he rode and came to know in which taverns along the coast the musicians gathered. On blustery nights, they sat near the iron stove and forewent talk of woe or politics, the music steady and only the wind out of key.

————

The wedding was set for October, and Albert gave him land to build a house. Joseph started the frame, trying to picture his own father choosing timbers for rafters, purlins, and joists, or for the tie beam. No image came, no knowledge of how he might have been. Joseph caught himself working too hard, panting. He clutched at his arms as if injured.

The dreams returned, and he recalled voices now. Children speaking their unknown tongue, gaunt women with parched lips.

Observing Félicité's life, he tried to see his place here. Her mother had died when she was young, and she'd raised her siblings. When she spoke of church and schooling, he heard his own mother and felt his life was written, as inevitable as the rhythm of a song.

When her sisters asked for stories of his travels, he said he had none.

———

A week before the wedding, he came into his room at the boarding house and in the dark a figure stood by the window, against the moonlight. His heart was suddenly pounding, his back damp with sweat.

"Félicité," he said, almost gasping her name when he recognized her.

It was the Sunday night before his last mail run as a single man. He went to her, and she placed her palms on his heaving chest.

"We could do it now," she told him.

"No," he said, startled, this so unlike her. "We have to wait."

"We are already married in my heart."

She took his cold hand and held it to her cheek. The pale light made the skin about her eyelids seem thin, almost amphibian. She moved his palm to her throat and along her shoulder.

"I'll be home soon," he whispered.

"I know."

She glanced at the window, her silhouette a recollection of his mother washed out against the sea's broad, carrying light. She'd gazed out and said, "He's not coming back. I can feel it."

"What are you thinking?" Félicité asked. "You are so silent."

She leaned close and her lips brushed his ear. Just before she spoke, in her open mouth, like a shell, was the sound of the ocean.

———

He rode steadily, not stopping for meals, the horse quick with his disquiet. The sky was marine blue, rock faces visible where downpours had stripped foliage. Corn ripened and yellowed. Men toiled in the earth, cutting furrows and filling baskets with potatoes. The air smelled of freshly turned fields and sweet smoke from chimneys, and with the nearing of the autumn equinox, high tide flooded coastal roads, leaving pale socks of salt on the horse's legs when they dried.

He passed his usual inn that afternoon and kept on through the evening, covering almost half of his route by nightfall. Riding in full dark, he left the gulf and followed a narrow lane between mountains. The horse was breathing hard, its head hung low.

Sometime past midnight he came to a small barn of freshly scythed hay set well away from the farm, beyond a rise and clearly just for extra fodder. He tethered the horse and watered it and carried the mail and communion wine inside. There was a lamp on the beam above the door, and he lit it and set it at his feet. Though the air was cold, he had begun to perspire.

He took out his fiddle and stood and played, the barn likely too far from the house for them to hear, and he not caring. He searched through melodies—the thousands of songs that had grown into each other, planted in his ear—as if for a single true sound, a human note.

He sweated hard, chest and back soaked. Between songs he uncorked a bottle of church wine. He moved the bow over the strings, stopped, and took the bottle again.

He played, pausing only to drink, one bottle and the next, until he was sawing madly, turning and stumbling, his eyes streaming from the dust rising at his feet and his chest aching, another continent lodged in it.

The lamp's wick burned low, guttering, tossing up black puffs, though the amber chamber was full. Shadows leapt, orange light lapping the walls. Cinder filled his nostrils, the smell suddenly familiar.

Holding the fiddle by its neck, he staggered back and then lunged and kicked the lamp. It struck the wall, spilling flame into the hay.

He walked outside as fire engulfed the barn. The horse rolled its eyes, broke its tether, and raced into the forest.

It was a cold night. He found himself staggering along a path, his fiddle in one hand, bow in the other. He walked until sunlight flashed with the wind in the trees, and beyond the cleft hills, the sea shone.

He wasn't far from the Baie des Chaleurs, and he kept to the woods. He walked on the paths only at night, carrying a stick to fend off dogs. He crossed the New Brunswick line the next day and went more slowly, stopping to eat now that no one was likely to recognize him.

In Caraquet, he studied the fishing town of clapboard houses not all that different from the others he'd known. At the docks he found passage to Prince Edward Island. Afraid of being tracked through shipping records, he gave his name as Joseph Mailloux.

The man with the pen looked up.

"Related to the Mailloux clan here?" he asked.

"Yes," Joseph told him. "Of course."

———

His mother didn't leave her chair to greet him. White streaked the hair that hung against her shoulders.

All that fall and winter he lived with her, keeping the house, taking work when it was to be had. Alone, he went to the shore and in the gulf air, beneath a clear, brittle sky, he sounded out the song. As if to force an answer from the music, he played until his fingers ached, trying to want nothing else, moving the bow along the strings, wearing away at the silence. When he stopped, waves fell loudly against the rocks, the sound as if within him, as if his life, this face, this self were but water through which he would fall.

The years passed in this fashion, his mother no longer complaining of his music but asking him to stay in the house, to keep her company on the winter days when he had time for his fiddle. He refused invitations to dances or bars and instead played for her. Sometimes, as he did, he saw what Félicité had the day she'd met him on the shore—a sailor in salt-bleached clothes, skin burned by sun and wind—and knew she'd be better off without him.

Once, at the docks, he heard his story told. Five years had passed since Rivière-au-Renard. The fishermen were smoking in the evening, talking as Joseph was about to leave.

"Here's a funny one," a sailor recently arrived from Gaspé said. "It's from back before my wife died and I went to sea. *Y avait un gar*—a fellow whose job it was to carry communion wine from town to town, a mailman. He rode through la Gaspésie."

Joseph paused. The man spoke of the fiancée and the mailman who rode as he fiddled—an odd sight.

"Who knows what his reasons were? He didn't seem to care about much more than his fiddle. He burned a barn. Some said he was drunk on communion wine, others that he'd found something of value in the mail and stolen it—a high crime." And then he said, "Pursued," as if the word didn't quite have meaning—"pursued by the Queen." Though there was a king on the throne, the Victorian expression remained.

"The constables came and asked about him. *Poursuivre par la reine*, we all said. *Il va se faire poursuivre par la reine.*"

The fishermen shook their heads, and one changed the subject to the war in Europe, the U-boat campaign and the brutal news that reached them weekly—Ypres, Loos, Verdun.

The third year of the war, Joseph's seventh winter home, his mother could barely stand. Each summer, she began to recover, but winter gripped her lungs. He carried her to her chair or bathed her silvery skin and lifted her back into bed.

Some nights, she called to him. "Play for me. I cannot sleep."

He fiddled, testing the limits of sound. It wasn't that the music made him feel human, but rather not—as if he were something else, a better animal.

One January evening, she told him how Louis had played for her when she was a child. Two years older, he'd fiddled as she danced about. She'd suffered jealousy the first time he'd fallen in love. Closing her eyes, she spoke softly. All those years, when he was a child, she was still a girl—seventeen when she'd become pregnant—a girl stranded on a foreign island and who chose not to return home.

"Why didn't you go back?" he asked. "There was nothing keeping us here."

"I refused to be pathetic in anyone's eyes. Here, I have a house, and people know my story and respect it. There, I'd have been a girl who ran off with a worthless man and returned to her parents. I loved that damned useless Irish father of yours, and I didn't want anyone but me to speak of him with scorn."

———

Ice melted from the coast, and the sea was alive again, salt on the wind. Spring passed. The muddy roads dried, and the air smelled of blossoms and cut grass.

His mother died one night in May. He placed her hands on her chest, over her Bible, and poured lamp oil onto the floor. He rolled the logs from the hearth, walked out with only the fiddle, and stood on the hill. He played his father's song.

The stars unfurled, suddenly faint as the fire lifted, darkening the road. Flames like orange curtains billowed up from the windows.

A small crowd gathered. They came from nearby farms and the village.

"What have you done?" a man asked.

Joseph lowered the fiddle. "She died."

"So you did this?"

He didn't respond. The sea's dark was immense, expanding around the light.

"He's crazy," someone said. "He never liked her."

Joseph turned away and started walking, knowing that if he found the man who'd said that—if he looked at him now, he would kill him, and maybe others.

"We'll have you arrested," someone called, but Joseph didn't stop.

———

He signed on with a merchant ship as Louis Mailloux, concerned that a warrant had been put out for his arrest, and he worked his way to Boston. The Americans had entered the war in April, and he wanted to join before it was over, though not as a British subject. He'd give his mother that.

In Boston, he enlisted. "Forty-two," he told them, lying about his age, but the officer didn't seem to care, and months later, the army began drafting men as old as forty-five. Nights, crossing to France, he stood on deck, closing his eyes, feeling the dark void of the invisible ocean.

He'd heard that the war was unlike any other, thousands dying each day.

It was like nothing he could have imagined.

The cratered earth stretched out, flaring at night, fields heaving with explosions, dirt and trees cast into the sky. Immense shells disinterred bodies from the mud, flinging them into sight, only to bury them again.

By no grace of his own, he avoided injury, even at Belleau Wood, where Bosch machine gunners cut through American troops. In preparation for Saint-Mihiel, he carried supplies to the front lines, over wheel ruts and craters. In sight of the German salient, men with rifles and shovels dug in. The Germans' long-range artillery cracked beyond the horizon, shells striking camps and roadways and the stone houses of Thiaucourt, walls lifting, moving outward, and crashing like waves.

The day before the battle, clouds filled the sky. In the trenches, men wrote letters with pencil nubs, hunching over their laps like children, until it grew dark.

Joseph volunteered for watch, and on the broken lands of the front, he played. Germans took shots, but others cried out and the firing stopped.

———

When dawn infiltrated the east, a young man called to Joseph. He said he was Irish American and knew Joseph's song but had never heard it the way he played it.

Like the others on the front, Joseph had brought a sheet of metal roofing to shelter his hole from the rain. The soldier crawled out to his post, and they propped it at an angle above their heads. He asked where Joseph had learned the song.

"My father taught me. When I was boy. Before he disappeared."

On the dark front, distant artillery flashed, outlining shattered trees. The young man sat with his knees pulled up. Slowly, Joseph began telling the story of how, after his father left, his mother turned her rage against the song. The young man listened, and gradually, taken by an unfamiliar urge, Joseph let himself speak of the years he and his mother had held a difficult truce, of his departure for Africa, the war and the music he'd learned in his travels. He described Félicité, his job as a mailman and the fire, his mother's death.

"Does it make sense to you?" he asked after a pause.

"Does what make sense?" the young man said.

"If this were a story I was telling you about some fellow I'd heard about, how could I explain it all?"

As the sun's harsh, angled light struck them, the young man stared, long and evenly, taking him in. Then the sun rose into the clouds, and the gray air became palpable, gusting with drizzle.

"What could make a man live this life?" Joseph asked.

The other man was briefly silent and then motioned to the sodden, desolate front.

"Who can say why men do what they do?"

------

In the charge Joseph was reckless. Shells struck, the earth moving beneath his feet like the deck of a ship in a gale. Men fell midstride. Smoke rose in a wall. Shrapnel flitted. He dropped to his knees, pain in his chest. He opened his jacket on the small, deep wound and tore a piece from his shirt. He jammed it into the hole and gasped.

Then he took up his rifle and continued, guarding positions, firing when he could.

He came upon the young man from the night before, curled on the ground and covered in dirt, not far from the edge of a deep crater.

"Are you hurt?"

The man quivered, his hands shaking. Joseph inspected him.

"You're fine," he said, knocking dirt from the young man, who still couldn't stand. Joseph carried him back past the trenches to the medical tent.

He sat him on the ground just outside. The young man looked up, his blue eyes rolling in his head, his jaw chattering as he tried to speak.

"It's fine," Joseph said. "You can thank me later."

The young man began to weep, his whole body shaking.

------

Each day Joseph pulled back his coat to check the wound as a girl might look at a locket. He hadn't told anyone. The flesh became discolored. He was short of breath.

By the last day of the battle, the Germans had refortified their positions at Metz. Joseph was stationed near the new lines, and that night he walked out and drew the bow over the strings. A bullet whirred past, followed by the report. Men shouted in German and no one else fired as he steadied his arm and played.

After a while, from the far side, a violin's clear voice joined with his. They played, turning back on the melody, mixing and rising, the other searching where his song dropped, gathering it back as if to hold his aching arm.

Then he returned to the song, simple as it had been when he'd learned it.

His chest ached and he couldn't breathe. A mist was settling, cooling his skin and darkening the earth. When he could play no longer, he sat and put the violin in its case to protect it from the drizzle and held it in his arms.

He closed his eyes and lay back into silence.

# The Glass Ladder

—⋅◦⋅—

**W**e saw her come down this road, past the birch growing out of the foundation of the old spring house, and she may have paused briefly there, in the shadow, thin as it is. What she wanted none of us could imagine, but that face of hers, those Normand eyes bright under the hood of rags, passed over us. She followed the road like a beggar, as if to call out for leftovers or coins, but continued silently, her feet bleeding and her body wrapped in a tattered sheet. She dragged her gaze over everything—our farms, our house.

Maybe she was destined for her trials since birth. She'd been granted too many hardships, and though we have all known difficulties, hers were not honest labor, the rearing of children, or the hand on the plow, but the result of pride, and not just her own. A girl raised by a fool and a harlot, in a house half-brothel, half-convent—as divided as a Hebrew temple—she'd never had a true place. It was as if she'd been chosen, sanctified through tribulation—though we and, in truth, everyone in this village, have been tried like Job and purified through suffering in smaller ways. Still, we should have taken her in, or offered her something. We have never been wanting.

The least we could have done was make the boys leave her alone. They followed her to see what had become of her—madness, we were calling it then.

Emelisse, they shouted. None dared throw rocks. Then we'd have said something. But her eyes, they hadn't changed, and if anything, pain had made her more striking, had given her the look of a terrified bride, one who, perhaps, had yet to meet her groom. Emelisse, the boys taunted, and when she at last flinched and gave them the gaze they wanted, they backed away. Maybe they saw death in her eyes and couldn't hate her as they'd hoped, though she did look hateful, clutching the sheet over her rags, careful to cover that body of hers, when once you could have paid the price of a bonbon to see it. Well, no doubt the price wasn't so cheap. But she'd never had a chance to start right, brought up by only two mothers, each crazy in a different fashion.

It's an odd story, and there are a couple ways about it, though it basically ends up the same. Some parts never change and others are always different, so you know what to expect and yet look forward to hearing it again.

———

One of Emelisse's mothers was Félicité, daughter of Albert Dubé. She was tall and pale, the source of those Normand eyes, and had had another daughter with a drunkard postman years before. That child was conceived out of wedlock a week before the two were supposed to marry. A few of the old-timers recalled that the father had the same eyes, and a story made its way among us that he'd been Félicité's estranged brother, separated at birth, and had fled after their union, realizing the nature of their sin. Félicité gave her daughter an odd name, Riva, and raised her in isolation, in a small house on the Dubé farm, with a high view of the sea.

The girl grew up awkward, so lonely on that coast she married the first man who paid her any attention. That was Gilles Boulay—a typical Boulay, lanky and hardworking. Family broods were so large none of us clearly recall which one he was. She was sixteen, and she lived in town with Gilles for two years, but she failed to give him a child. Then he went to *la Nouvelle Angleterre*, for a job in a shoe mill in Nashua. He said he'd send for her but never did, and a year later, she went and found him, newly married with a pregnant wife. She stayed on as if to be a second wife, working as a hotel maid and living in a rooming house, accepting his visits. We knew this from relatives who emigrated.

It was madness, we told ourselves, an acceptance of immorality, and no doubt in her blood, in light of what happened next to Félicité.

———

Emelisse's second mother was Bibianne Miouse, granddaughter of Donald MacNeil, who, during *la drave*, when the men ran timber downriver, could pull out the corner of a logjam by himself and get things moving. She took after him, a squarish woman who wore her apron everywhere, except to church, and walked with kicking strides, swinging her arms like an angry child.

It was as if Emelisse's life were planned and the lives of others were sacrificed to bring her into this world. Whereas in the years after Riva left, Félicité had the earnest attention of every village man but unnaturally never grew ripe, Bibianne repeatedly miscarried with the exception of a baby boy, a tortured thing whose body twisted on itself until he died. Her husband and the dead boy's father was Arthur Miouse, *un vrai innocent*. He was handsome but foolish, pompous and without a trade, living on the graces of his father, a clothes merchant. Before his marriage to Bibianne, Arthur cuckolded many men, all the while courting little Lise Marceau, a beauty and not too brilliant herself. We'd been sure the two would make a couple until the day Bibianne announced that Arthur had gotten her pregnant. When he denied it—and *bon Dieu*, he denied it—she gave him a thrashing in front of the courthouse. He wasn't a small man either. We all enjoyed that.

So Arthur and Bibianne married, and to prove his son's worth, Arthur's father built them the biggest house in town, an ugly affair with columned porches that gathered snow and so many windows that heating the rooms must have been impossible.

Arthur and Bibianne came to church every Sunday, for she was so devout that if she'd let Arthur bed her out of wedlock, it was as near to a miracle as we'd seen. Had the Holy Virgin been as piously prude as Bibianne, and the Good Lord in his carnal form less seductive than Arthur, Jesus wouldn't have been conceived, and we would all still be pagans. But in the pews, Bibianne held Arthur's arm and squeezed it, not with affection but with wincing pressure each time his eye strayed to Lise Marceau or the narrow shoulders of another village girl. But though Bibianne kept him on a leash, she lost all her children, and, once, she grew in size until we were sure there were twins, but then—and we can all swear by this—she mysteriously became smaller, until she was normal sized, stomping out chores and swinging her arms above great broad steps through town.

All the while, Félicité lived alone in that little house above the sea. Her sisters and her daughter had moved away, and then her father died, and we began calling her *la veuve*—the widow. We didn't know who started that, but it suited her. Some of the old-timers have even gone so far as to say she briefly had a husband who died and who has since been forgotten, but that seems unlikely. Age has fogged their memories, and they must merely be recalling the death of her father who'd been a private, aloof man and the only person to assure her well-being.

But the strangest thing about Félicité was that she didn't age. Her beauty didn't dim. If anything, it grew. Unlike most of our women, who'd had a dozen or so children, she'd had just one and kept her figure. Her solitude had always seemed a sin, taking what God intended for matrimony and wasting it on seclusion. In her house that buckled beneath the snow and leaned away from the sea wind, she accepted a widow's fate, surviving on what men brought her during their secret nightly visits. There was even a traveling salesman, a gaunt figure with some Jew blood who stopped in on his trips. And, of course, there was Arthur.

On a July afternoon, Bibianne was coming down from the high fields up past Félicité's land. She'd been picking wild strawberries, and as she passed the house, she saw the bright green door on it. We all knew that a bear had broken into Arthur's new car garage—his father having bought him a Ford—and had stolen off with the leather seat cover. Arthur replaced the garage's side door, which the bear had cracked, and then installed it on Félicité's house, since it was still better than the rotten one she'd had. It was a door we would have recognized on a passing barge—banded, with a small square window, and paint as green as July.

The first time Bibianne saw the door on the house, she stood in the road, staring and trembling. Germain Dugas, who was returning home with a sack of freshly shot grouse, saw her, saw the basket of berries spill onto the dirt, and her face become as red as a wound.

She said something then, about a harlot, and went up the porch and knocked open the door. Sure enough, Arthur ran out naked. Bibianne wasn't fast enough to grab him, so she dragged Félicité out by her hair, shaking her so that it's a wonder her neck didn't snap. She'd meant to carry the sinner into town and strip her camisole—which was all Félicité had had time to get on—and beat her in front of everyone, but Félicité said—and Germain Dugas heard this—that she was pregnant and it was Arthur's.

So Bibianne carried her back inside and put her to bed, told her to stay put, as if that wasn't already where she spent most of her time. Then Bibianne went home, gathered her possessions, and returned to take care of Félicité. Right up until the birth of Emelisse, the two of them lived in that house.

Arthur wasn't seen again, though Onésime's cousin, down

working the mills in Hartford, said he'd read about his death in the paper. Arthur had been in Manhattan, dressed in pinstripes with a boutonniere of tiny pink roses—*that* was in the paper, Onésime told us. As Arthur came around a corner, he almost stepped on a skunk, right there, on *l'Avenue du Parc.* It sprayed him and he jumped away, into the street, and a taxi hit him. That's why it was in the paper, because it was a silly death and nobody had claimed the body. The police knew his name from the papers in his wallet.

Bibianne was generally accepted as a widow after that. Arthur had left with his money and car, but she sold the rest, even their parcel of land, though she had their house moved, board by board, and rebuilt next to Félicité's small, rotting home, so that she and Félicité could live together. Isolated from town, set on those empty hills above the sea, the immodesty of the house was clear—an extravagance, the exaggeration of qualities that should be kept to oneself.

————

We should have known from Emelisse's life, the odd events that might be read as signs, that she would be special. Curé Félix was running the parish then, and he hated Félicité, but what he did to Emelisse—even if she was the fruit of sin—was too cruel for a man of the cloth and had to be a test delivered from the divine hand which casts affliction and catastrophe.

The first we heard of Emelisse was from passersby on the road who saw Bibianne on the porch with a baby, but none heard the child cry, making us wonder if she had gone mad and was carrying about a doll, or worse—another stillborn. A few years later, when we walked the road near the Dubé farm, a dark-haired girl watched us from the brambly garden or from behind the pillars of the porch. Not long after, Bibianne began parading her through town, showing her off—startlingly pretty, with the blackest hair braided with such intricacy we didn't doubt the vanity in that home. Already then, the girl stared out with the awed eyes of a creature who never expected to see a world like ours. She didn't touch anything or speak, and in church, we watched her as the curé gave his sermon. Those eyes didn't seem to blink.

Her life was unimaginable to us. Our days were the same: the fields and the hunt, the steady readying for winter and the logging camps when the earth froze. Our children had lain in the same cradle that we had, been rocked on the same floor, heard the old stories and felt them on their own lips—the voices of uncles and grandfathers, nephews and sons.

But to have grown up in that house on the coast, to be fed by the lust of men who came at night, we could not imagine. The garden returned to forest. Branches scarred the house's walls when the sea wind blew. Stories of life inside came from Félicité's furtive lovers. Clément Singelais told us that men brought firewood and that when this ran low, Bibianne pulled boards off the small home Félicité had previously lived in, so that it disappeared slowly, devoured by the big house. A bedroom turned into a chicken coop, stocked with the hens men used as pay. A sitting room filled with poorly mended household goods cast off by village wives and brought by husbands. There was even a stained glass window, made by the same artisan who fashioned the new one for the church, and it hung where a storm blew out a grid of panes, above Félicité's bed.

We would pass in the road and see Bibianne reading to Emelisse from the Bible, each few words staggered with pauses, since she'd never been quick. Félicité still didn't age, enduring the way hermits do in their solitude, her beauty enlivened by her absence from our lives since we pictured her from stories but never saw her up close. Maybe nothing could impede her desire after so long without a husband, but why Bibianne didn't throw the men out, we weren't sure. She'd understood something about the hand of God, or she simply couldn't hate anything about Félicité, not after she'd given her the child she'd so desired.

Emelisse became tall and slender, with eyes like sunlit water, and though she was pious enough, attending every Mass, we saw what she did in the fields above the sea. All of us observed it sooner or later. It might have been dancing. We'd witnessed nothing like it. She hopped and turned in the tall grass like an injured bird, her arms extended. She pranced on wide, flat ridges of stone, silhouetted against the curving sea. She spun and leapt, moving her arms in strange shapes. We could attach no meaning to her motions. No one here could have taught her this. We understood why the curé hated her.

As she grew, she spent more time performing her mad rituals, even in the snow. We began to see who her real mother was from the sway of her hips, how she smoothed her skirt to her thighs before sitting, or even how she carried her gaze over and past men, as if they weren't there, but so that they could look upon her face. She wore a simple necklace, a silver chain, and when she neared workers on the road or young men by a splitting stump, she moved her fingers past her throat and lifted the simple cross from between her breasts. Some said she'd been too isolated to understand. Bibianne had guarded her, stepped in front of people who tried to speak with her, and even struck Onésime's golden spaniel dead when it growled at Emelisse in the street.

After killing the dog, Bibianne lost sensation in her fingers. Her hand curled into a permanent fist and withered. Not long after, she began to tremble, her jaw shaking and her hair going gray.

One dawn, a grave appeared on the hillside above the sea. We tried to imagine Félicité and Emelisse digging that hole in the unsanctified earth, though we saw neither do so—only Emelisse performing her vexing dance around it. Soon after, we were shocked to encounter Bibianne shuffling along the road, her good hand bandaged from the shovel. Félicité's soul had fled to the source of her passions. We couldn't imagine how, though some speculated that her soul had aged cruelly and died even though her body persisted with its tawdry charms.

———

Even as a young woman, Emelisse didn't speak to anyone in town or stop at the church to pray alone, as we do, kneeling in the pews, hoping that winter will be gentle or the corn too high to see the elderberry at the fence lines. We have argued over this late at the table, until the meat turned cold and clotted in our throats, even though we had to wake soon, to feed pigs and cows, carry the plow into the fields, or burn out stumps and vines. Cutting back weeds, we have all been alone with our memories of what she became at the end of her life—that barefoot wretch, leaving prints of blood on the dusty road, shapeless beneath her sheet but for the stories the men told of how she danced herself to shame in the city, for money, under colored lights. We've had to ask if our own suffering could do what hers eventually did—crack a church foundation or bring snow out of an August sun.

One source of her confusion, we understood, was simply that Bibianne had kept her from us. Emelisse had grown up without friends her own age. Passing in the street, she stared at the games of children as if they were the ceremonies and intrigues of courtly society. We knew this but didn't understand the power of her estrangement until the autumn she met Magloire Fortin.

Magloire—this is how his father, Onésime, tells it—idealized her, had seen her sitting on her faraway porch, her back against a cracked pillar, reading, or in her trance of wild, provoking movements in the field. As is to be expected of a boy in the heat of his teenage years, he'd imagined a profound, lonely, and inventive girl—had, in short, imagined her. Magloire was handsome, much as Onésime had been—tall and broad shouldered—but unlike his father, he was dreamy. He wrote poetry and told people openly how the church had hidden great works of art.

Onésime, being the mayor at that time, warned him to keep opinions private, not for fear of trouble—there's no real trouble to be had in opinions—but out of respect for the congregation and caution for the sharp tongue of Curé Félix. The worst thing that could happen to any of us was to have the curé deliver a sermon about something we'd done or failed to do. But Magloire claimed, back then at least, that he was guided by his heart. Since Bibianne was now unable to leave the house, Emelisse went alone to the store once a week and spoke only the single words that identified each of the items she needed. Magloire walked up to her, cavalier in plain sight of the men gathered at Anctil's store, and asked her to the harvest dance.

Onésime, who saw the whole thing from the oak bench on the store's porch, said she held Magloire's face with those unblinking eyes. The wind didn't move her hair or ripple her clothes, though the sign above Anctil's doorway creaked on its chains. Other than this and the wind itself, the silence was complete.

According to the others on the porch, Magloire blushed at the show he'd given the village men and was turning away when she said, *Yes*. But Réjean Fournier, who'd also been on the porch, said Emelisse was the one who blushed and drew her hands up to her chin, her arms over her breasts.

What? she asked and then, Why? as if Magloire's proposal were inconceivable.

The harvest dance, he repeated, pleased, according to Réjean, by her timidity. He took the opportunity to step close, his face an inch from hers, and spoke quietly toward her lips—words nobody heard because of Gérald Coulombe's almost incessant blathering about the hockey game he'd heard on the radio the day before. It was only when she left and Onésime asked Magloire that they all found out she'd agreed to go.

At first, Onésime forbade the match. Magloire said a rose can't be blamed for growing among briars. Onésime invoked common sense, madness, inheritance, and then simply shouted, No! so loudly that he startled the baby next door into a fit of crying. For all of Magloire's dreaminess, he was as hardheaded as his father. Onésime found endless tasks for his son on the family's land and in the courthouse. To make sure that Magloire didn't scamper off, Onésime worked side by side with him, occasionally pausing to ask him if he could abandon his notions about the girl though Magloire refused to respond. Only after having reinforced the sagging rafters of the barn, rebuilt a stone fence where frost heaves had broken it, and sanded and varnished the courtroom floor, did Onésime relent. He let Magloire sleep the two days before the dance.

Onésime drove to Campbellton, in Nouveau-Brunswick, to the house of Adélard Carrier. Onésime was frank, as he had little time. He showed papers relating to the family legacy and presented his friend with a leather pouch of bank notes. The deal was made. Adélard's daughter Brigitte was a known beauty and also intelligent. Though Adélard had worked out a way for her to be schooled near Boston, in a place called Wellesley, Onésime sold his friend on her new future. Of course, Réjean Fournier, who had family in Campbellton, told us that American schooling was simply one of her fantasies and that her father was in fact pressuring her to marry Patrick Gordon, an aging, well-to-do Scots merchant. Onésime arrived just in time, and since she had fond memories of playing hide-and-seek with Magloire on a visit years before, she agreed to the match.

Onésime returned with Brigitte at dawn, well before Magloire awoke from his long adolescent sleep. She waited among the trees at the edge of a field until Onésime, as a signal, swept the porch and stairs. She came up the road. The hem of her skirt was wet from crossing the field, her hands and face flush with cold. She knocked.

Get that, Onésime called, and Magloire, having just come down-stairs, opened the door on an apparition of beauty and despair. My parents, she said, and then held back a sob, they've drowned. She fell into his arms. He later realized that she was a friend of the family, that they shared childhood memories of hiding in a cornfield and of chaste kisses under a purpling, stormy dusk. He learned that her parents had gone down in a ship just outside the port of Dalhousie. Later, when she was calm and they sat together on the couch, she confided in him—as Onésime had schooled her to do—that the most beautiful works of art were surely kept hidden by the church.

Brigitte had a fair complexion and was pleasantly confident, so that walking the road or at work in the house, she appeared at ease. That harvest dance, we chose her as queen, and she was a joyous one, as she'd discovered that her parents weren't dead, but that another ship had capsized and the reports had been confused. She'd told Magloire that her pain had been as real as if they'd died and his kindness had healed her.

As the fiddlers played, she danced in and out of Magloire's arms. A warm wind blew up from the south, pushing the cold out to sea, and new clouds covered the moon. Briefly, in the shift of climates, flurries fell, the snow almost warm, catching in our hair and melting before it touched the ground. The bonfire's sparks trailed into the sky. More than one child was conceived that night, and a few marriages ensued. Even the confessional and Curé Félix seemed welcoming. We all looked to Brigitte as she moved among us, snow melting on her cheeks.

Her smile faltered only when Emelisse came to the edge of the circle. The musicians stopped. She wore a black dress with cutaway shoulders and flaps below the arms. She must have made it from an obsolete garment, inspired by a magazine clipping. It was sepulchral and yet obscene, a dress that might have been worn for a dead matri-arch's vigil but refashioned for a nightwalker. Even worse was how she entered the circle. She moved the way she did in the fields, her arms lifted as she turned in strange, prancing steps.

In the old stories, it is the devil who interrupts the dance and takes the village's prettiest daughter into his arms as the instruments leap involuntarily to life in the musicians' hands. He holds his palm to her back and it burns itself there as they dance, faster and faster, until he lets her drop with a wound that will never heal. We must have all shared this thought as she encroached. Red-faced, she stopped her dance, sensing our fear or hearing muffled gasps and laughter. Her eyes reflected the firelight, as empty as those of a frightened horse.

Brigitte took Magloire's hand and stepped forward and said loudly, Go away!

A baby began to cry, and Roger Chouinard, a barrel-chested and already balding country boy who was soon to take charge of his ailing father's potato farm, said, Wait. Dance with me.

She looked past him, at Magloire, and then ran clumsily away, into the shadow ringing the fire. The folds of cloth below her arms flapped like wings.

———

It wasn't long afterward that Emelisse spoke with the curé and told him, in a soft, disjointed voice, that she'd decided to become a nun.

Curé Félix had always disliked the women on that farm, even Bibianne. They were the town's scandal—a sign that he hadn't fully conquered his parish. He'd long had the habit of spitting into his handkerchief. In public, when faced with someone he didn't like—village boys who smoked at the maple shacks or men who bought whiskey from passing ships—he pulled the handkerchief from his pocket, snapped it open, and held it before him, directly in front of the person's face. With the two corners pinched in his fingers, he spat into it, the wad of phlegm striking the thin cloth.

Clouds had brought evening early that day. Édouard Labrie was on his way to pray for his youngest, who suffered fits. As he opened the church door, he heard the shouts—the curé's voice distended, breathless with anger, like wind hissing through the rocks and tall grass along the shore.

Standing penitent, Emelisse endured the old curé's rage until he did the trick with his handkerchief. Then she spun and ran past Édouard, pushed open the heavy door, clutching her shawl at her throat. The curé himself fled, into his quarters so quickly that Édouard was left alone, squinting into the musty dark. No candles burned in the nave. We all noticed, at the next Mass, the fissure rising between the hewn stones, though a few claimed the foundation had been washing out for years.

Édouard—and he is an honest, hardworking man—told us what he'd seen: her thin, startled figure below the sudden dark of clouds, her slim arms and shins as she ran, her shawl snapped from her grip and twisted up along the wind, and the church door, a slab of engraved oak that, in the gusting silence of her flight, fell shut behind her.

———

Perhaps, we said, God made us reject her so she could come to her trial and suffer gloriously. It seemed we had hated her, yet we couldn't say we'd known her. She was an empty glass, ready to receive what the world put into it.

Early next Sunday—how this happened none of us understands—a cream-colored Chrysler Imperial drove into town. The driver was a young man named Jack Beetle, an American, he said, and he told us in good French that he'd come for Emelisse. He was pale, in a pink shirt that might have been silk, and his hair and eyes and suit shone black like the polished leather of a whip. Some said that no exhaust came from his car's muffler. Clément Singelais swore that the air from inside was as cold as winter.

While we made our way to church, the Chrysler drove through town and disappeared up the road to the farms along the coast. That evening, Bibianne came into town raving. She smashed a bench and tore up a hitching post, and when men tried to calm her, she threw them down. According to Laurent Pelletier, the men followed her shouts into the woods and after many struggles fixed up a sort of halter that they used to drag her back to her house. They said that when they brought her into those empty rooms, she collapsed. It seems now that was also the night Onésime had his stroke, though he survived. The next day, Curé Félix consented to burying Bibianne in the church plot, since, of those women, she'd been the only one without sin. During the Mass, he was haggard, coughing, his handkerchief in his fist.

At first, we wondered what happened to Emelisse. Some said she had, in fact, gone to a convent, but Réjean Fournier's boy, who is rumored to own a few books forbidden by the Index, said—and he said this in public, right in front of Anctil's store—that she'd gotten the hell out of this town and who could blame her? We heard about that from the pulpit, three Sundays running. But more quietly, we wondered if there was something we could have done, if we'd been too harsh, and it did seem, when word finally got around that she was dancing in the cabarets, that we were relieved not to have been wrong about her.

It must have been two or three months after she left that Samuel Boudreau brought a load of soapstone down from Montréal. He swore he'd seen a girl in a cabaret who looked like Emelisse, though she had a different name. She was dancing on a stage in that way of hers—he recognized it from the field—or, when others danced, she was sitting next to Jack Beetle—at least, it sounded like him—his black-gloved hand on her thigh.

It was around that time that Edgar Chassé, a childhood friend

of Magloire's, returned from France—one of the few men we knew
who'd gone and survived Normandy. He'd arrived in Montréal
with fellow soldiers. They were celebrating the end of the war and
their return home, and he invited Magloire to join them. Brigitte
was furious with his sudden trip, what with the chores to be done
since the birth of their son, but already then, even before the accident, Magloire was changing.

Magloire was the one to tell Edgar about Emelisse, and of
course Edgar remembered her and had to see what she'd become
with his own eyes. During his nights celebrating in the city, he
met a fellow in show business who knew where she danced. She
was going by the name Anastasie Angélique. Edgar and Magloire
later told us what happened next but in their own ways, which is
normal, since Magloire came back blind and Edgar took to the
bottle and moved south to *les States*.

In the company of the former soldiers, the two friends had
waited outside the club—not really a cabaret after all but a far
worse place, if that's possible. Magloire told them about Emelisse—
her strangeness and beauty, her harlot mother, her isolation on that
coastal farm—until soon they all felt they'd known her. But when
she arrived with Jack Beetle, her city garments almost made her
unfamiliar again. She moved with confidence. The wind molded
her blouse as if of her own will.

They followed her inside. The other girls in the club appeared
distant and mysterious under the lights, but the soldiers, having
heard stories of Emelisse, felt she was one of theirs. Edgar told the
club owner he'd grown up with her and when Jack Beetle came
out, they paid him so they could be alone with her in a room.
Our boys wanted to celebrate the victory for which they'd risked
their lives, and as for Emelisse, she'd chosen a certain role, not so
different from that of Félicité. We have since forgiven our men who
took the night road to her farm.

Edgar said that the party was all in good humor. They wanted her to dance the way she had in the field, and she did—brashly, nothing of the shy girl left. She gave them a show, taunting them with the movement of her shoulders or moving her thigh through the slit in her dress. They wanted her best trick and pooled their money.

What she did looked almost penitent, Edgar said, and Magloire agreed. She dropped her gaze and slipped her arms from the straps of her dress. She held her chest and knelt, and then lowered her palms as if with an offering, or in penitence.

Edgar said he would have paid for that alone. When asked, Magloire grunted his assent. But the soldiers wanted more. They'd been to France and Germany, corrupted by the desperate acts of hopeless women.

No one recalls how she ended up doing the trick. The idea must have been her own. It was something involving two bottles. She pulled off her dress. The men fell silent. Not even they expected this—a performance with two long-neck beer bottles that she took from the men's hands and emptied onto the floor. They all noticed how she wasn't looking at them but staring at the back of the room, to where Jack Beetle sat, as if she were doing this for him. He just watched, a cigarette in his fingers, his pale face dressed in smoke.

Edgar swears that he looked away as she turned her back to them and put the bottles partway into her body, one and then the other. When she released them, they hung there. Then, for the soldiers' amusement, she jerked her hips, and the bottles knocked together, clanking. Their round bottoms faced the men, not quite like eyes. Their scuffed ends were as dull as nail heads.

Edgar did get cut that night. He'd survived Germany without a scratch only to be gashed along the side of his neck—a pale mark, not yet faded in the days before he went south. But it was Magloire whose eyes received the shards. He'd been at the edge of the stage, staring up at her thighs and back, which he might have

experienced as a husband, when she jerked her hips even more violently—as if, as some of the men said, she were experiencing the
only intimacy she'd ever known. Magloire saw the bottles come
together—and then the splintering air.

If Edgar is to be believed, Magloire leapt back in pain, his eyes
bleeding as he swung his fists blindly, attacking everyone in the
bar. He tried, he grudgingly admitted on one of his nights when
he'd had too much to drink, to kill Jack Beetle who'd brought this
curse upon all of us. In his agony he accidently struck another
soldier, and a small tussle broke out—nothing unusual for soldiers,
playful, in fact, Edgar told us. But somehow she was knocked from
the stage, and with those shards in her. That's the only way the
men could explain what happened next. In the high spirit of their
victory in Europe, they hadn't realized she'd been luring them into
a moment that would harm so many lives.

We have since seen Magloire weep on his porch, blind to those
who pass as he recalls the shards falling into his eyes like tears denied for so long that, condensed and resilient, they came to possess
the cutting obstinacy of diamonds. Edgar told us that, in the moment before she fell from the stage, she stood like a naked child,
bleeding like a woman, her face transpierced with passion, like
sunlight through stained glass. And when she came through town,
that dirt-stained sheet covering her rags, she sometimes paused.
In those places, there was blood, gathered along the insides of her
feet, the half prints more like a forgotten scriptural mark than the
trace of a passing woman.

Magloire rarely speaks about all this. His children are grown
and do not visit him, and Brigitte died young. They have said
that he beat them like no other parent in our town. When he was
angered, he reached about him frantically and caught one of them
by the hair or shirt and then struck them with clumsy blows to the
face and chest until he exhausted himself. It was the blindness that
changed him.

———

When Emelisse returned that August, we first mistook her for one of the beggars who goes village to village, door to door. Some claimed it wasn't even her, but others saw her face—those eyes—and remembered her. She never stopped, not after night fell, not even as she passed her old house above the sea.

Clément Singelais, who'd been caring for the abandoned land, saw her on the road. She was muttering to herself in the way of people who have lost their minds or have been alone for too long, though she spoke of a dream—a narrow ladder of glass that tore at her flesh and led to a garden. Each night, before she reached it, she grew weak from loss of blood and slipped from the rungs and woke.

When she came through the village, Eude Pelletier, drunk as usual, followed her, as did a few boys. When Clément told the story of the ladder, Eude said this was what he'd overheard her mumbling—how each night she danced around a garden spring where she saw someone from the village drinking: Magloire to heal his eyes, Curé Félix to soothe his lungs that made climbing to the pulpit a struggle, and others, even Eude himself. The last time she had the dream, after climbing those lacerating rungs, she found herself in a garden where a shepherd gave her the milk he took from a sheep. She awoke with sweetness on her lips, knowing she had only to wear out her days here—never sleeping again, never climbing in her dreams. As she spoke those words to herself, she passed here, on this road, right there, through the thin shadow of that birch.

The boys said that, when she left the coast, a path opened in a dense forest between mountains and closed upon them as they followed, so that they were lost for a day and a night. With the constable's help, we searched for them from the road to where the land meets the sea and into the mountains on the other side.

All that night, the hounds of Germain Dugas bayed, and in the mornings, birds wheeled above treetops—large, dark shapes slow against the wind. A hunter dozed in the woods and dreamed her with a crown of shards.

In the forest, a shrine appeared—a lean-to of sticks, hung with rags, the rocks around it decorated with smashed beer bottles. Some say it was a schoolboy prank, others that it is dedicated to the Fair Penitent. There has been discussion among us about which day Emelisse disappeared—in August or rather in July, on the day of the Magdalene.

When we tell her story now, we nod, but the grandchildren do not understand. They have been to the city. They disdain the stony fields, the compulsion of sun and season, or have simply never known it, eager as they are for easy work.

Among us, there are still some who dream glassy air suspended like a ladder. The boys who followed her have grown but they tell us that when she lay down in the forest, on the stones, crystal snow fell from the warm sky like the blossoms of a shaken tree.

# III

(1910–1982)
FRANCE
THE UNITED STATES
MEXICO

# Protest Song

— I —

She sat on the edge of the bed, her knees together, and then reached down and took off her shoes. She placed them next to the package of rations he'd given her. Her dark eyes followed the motions of her hands, never once looking at him. She removed her wool jacket. As she unbuttoned her blouse, the cold gave her gooseflesh on the backs of her arms. He had been standing but got onto his knees as she took off her brassiere.

He lifted his hands and held them inches from her breasts, as if warming himself at a fire. She had a small, angular nose and bobbed, black hair pinned to the side with a steel barrette.

"*Je t'aime*," he said, the only words he knew aside from *bonjour* and *au revoir*, and for the first time since he'd brought the rations to her door, she glanced at his face.

A distant, shrill whistling began, and she cried out, covering her head with her arms. The earth boomed, and the small window blew inward, spraying them with glass. The floor bucked like the deck of a ship.

In the ringing silence, a faint cracking sound began, reminiscent of river ice under his feet. A line of sky appeared above them. The stone wall behind the bed peeled away, tilted, and collapsed into a crater.

"*Non, non!*" she shouted and jumped up. Soldiers and townspeople gathered, some tending to the fallen, others staring into the room: the young, half-naked Frenchwoman shaking her fists.

In the street, a towheaded soldier shot his arm up.

"Hey!" he said. "Hey! I was next in line."

—

Reader, the story of Nolan's virginity is a long one, and not as odd as you might think for a man of his time. He was a different breed of American from today's aging virgin whose libido has burned up with his avatars, in dark rooms, alone in the waxy light of an LCD screen. No great believer in much of anything, Nolan was raised to fear authority and lacked the courage to go outside social constraints, though he could find no way to live within them. His life was not a comedic film—no spoof on the awkward man-boy, nerd sci-fi collector—but the slow anguish of a broken body and unwilled solitude.

Nor was Nolan made for war, and the war knew it. Since his arrival in France, the distant artillery had begun tracking him. He felt the first impact in his bones before the dark plume lifted from a field. A second followed, thirty feet away, killing three and wounding five. Those first days, when the rare long-range shell struck, it was savagely close. The dead had stood nearby, and he'd seemed fortunate, but soon men avoided him. He had yet to see combat, and already soldiers were calling him No Luck Nolan.

A cold, penetrating rain fell the night that his company advanced, dragging sheets of metal roofing. Across the front, howitzers flared. Since March, the Germans' biggest gun had been lobbing two-hundred-pound shells seventy miles into the streets of Paris. Troops had discussed the Big Berthas that could hurl twenty-five-hundred-pound explosive shells and the Langer Maxes whose twenty-eight-mile shots pitted the rear front. On the horizon, Bosch observation balloons loomed: a series of immense, disembodied heads.

His fellow soldiers told him to keep his distance as they dug in. Most of them visited prostitutes often, but fearing hellfire, he'd waited too long. And from what he'd seen of the steadier soldiers, hellfire must be tonifying indeed. They were manly and savvy, joking about the enemy, about their hardship, grunting with confidence. Alone, he shivered as he dug at the mud. He pictured artillery shells high above, each one sniffing out his vestal spoor with the nose of a hound before plummeting toward him.

That night, as he huddled beneath the sheet metal, a soldier began to play the violin. The buzzing in Nolan's sternum softened and then dissipated. He placed the song: a simple tune his father whistled from time to time, unusually melancholy for a man who showed so much strength.

The music lasted through the night, the same melody returning, until dawn moved along the horizon, dark as a lead seam. Nolan crawled over the mud and whispered, "Hey," before slipping into the violinist's shelter. He'd expected a young soldier, with delicate fingers and the gaze of a child, but the man was at least forty, with a look of muscular endurance and eyes as blue as broken ice.

Nolan told him that he knew another version of the song from his father. After some hesitation, Joseph—the violinist—described how his own father, a fisherman on Prince Edward Island, taught it to him before drowning at sea. He spoke of a childhood in Canada, between two cultures—French and English—and his abandonment of his home to fight in an earlier colonial war. The story went on, a litany of violence and failure closing with the abandonment of a woman—his certainty that he was too animal, too broken and unpredictable to give her a good life—and then his arrival on this cratered earth.

"What could make a man live this life?" Joseph asked, and the emptiness in his words—that a man far older than Nolan could speak this way—terrified him.

———

When the charge began, Nolan was shaking. Men lay slashed by machine gun fire, arms splayed. A soldier in his outfit was missing his bottom half, still moving, like a crab. Nolan's legs went to rubber and he vomited.

Then the final shell detonated. He came to, sitting in mud, sobbing so hard his jaw chattered. He'd urinated. His head moved as if worked by a ratchet, but his chest held still, his spine rigid, pegged to the earth.

Joseph jogged past with his rifle, stopped and turned back. He crouched. His face was pale, flecked with mud. He had blood on his chest. He moved his mouth as a ringing grew to a pitch in Nolan's ears. He slung Nolan's rattling body over his shoulders and carried him back past the trenches to the medical tents.

After checking him for wounds—the only blood on his uniform was from Joseph—the medical staff flung him onto a cot. There were no sounds save those in his dreams: the whistling of shells that no skill or intelligence could predict. If he tried to move even his finger, the tremor echoed throughout his body, resonating, amplifying, until he thrashed. Maybe the explosion had incinerated his nerves. The fits lasted until sweat soaked him and he passed out, back into the war all over again.

Maybe it was a day, or two or three days, later that soldiers carried Joseph into the medical tent. He clutched his violin case. His skin was gray. A doctor checked for a pulse and then pried the case from his arms. He opened his jacket and shirt. There was a dark wound just above his right nipple. The doctor covered the body.

The possessions of the dead rarely stayed around for long. Though moving a finger had been devastating, Nolan eased himself up from the fetal position. That alone must have taken fifteen minutes. He closed his eyes. The war rumbled behind them even when he was awake. He saw himself on the front, soldiers firing from trenches as the whistling grew louder. The medical tent shook and swayed. Clods of dirt rained down on it. The doctor and nurses ran outside.

Nolan put his foot down. It struck the wooden slats of the floor. With a motion like falling, he swung the other foot over and threw his body after it.

Step by step, he advanced in a half-squat, arms out like wings, fingers typing the air. Sweat turned cold on his face and neck and chest. His bladder released, his legs pleasantly hot and then growing numb. He fell forward, sprawling across the floor. One arm hooked the case and pulled it close, as if the comfort in the song lived inside the violin.

When Nolan woke again, he was back on the cot, the case locked in his arms. His body was a seismic mess, seizures like skirmishes along the highways of his limbs.

For a few more days, Nolan remained unscathed in this lineup of broken men who looked as if they'd picked a fight with a pork butcher and lost in a different way. It disgusted him that he could not control his body. The doctor who examined him before issuing the release papers mirrored his revulsion. Sneering, he opened and closed his lips.

Six months later, when Nolan saw his father's expression, his hearing had returned and he could imagine what the doctor had said.

"Not wounded?"

His father stood on the porch in the brisk late November air, as if not yet sure he should invite his son inside.

Nolan had had no news from his father since a letter announcing his mother's death from influenza. He hadn't been able to hold a pen, and even on days when his nerves were steady, the thought of explaining his discharge gave him convulsions.

He struggled to describe what had happened.

"That's not a wound," his father said. "That's sickness."

He stopped, half-turned in the doorway.

"My God, boy, did you even get through a single battle?"

———

Nolan's father, Francis Myron Sheridan, was the son of Nolan Myron Sheridan, a Civil War veteran who'd lost a hand when a cannonball skipped across the turf at Manassas and who'd later shot and cremated a taxman, single-handedly. Francis Myron Sheridan had himself known hardship: one of twelve children who fought for primacy, labored in the fields, fell crippled from polio and toppling trees, died of diseases and snakebite, or went to war on the plains. Francis Sheridan had fought starving, Indigenous tribes and, on church days, wore his medal of honor as well as a bone watch fob made from the kneecap of a black man he'd helped lynch.

Yes, reader, I know. Before you decide this man is a monster and interpret this story as an easy moral tale of a generational dichotomy, remember that he was a monster of his time (in a time of monsters). Many people liked having a piece of a murdered person whose humanity they denied. They mailed parts to each other, shot postcards of families posing with the corpse, and fashioned souvenirs from bones. The golden age of stringing up a black man for looking crosswise at a white woman appeared to be on the wane, but if Nolan found such things revolting, it was due to the sensitive constitution that Francis Sheridan derided and not his enlightened ethics.

But maybe there is also a little truth to the generational divide. Francis Sheridan was a big man, no longer burly in arm and leg, but retaining the barrel chest of one who has breathed hard in cold air and snored loudly by the fire. And his head had a boulder-like quality to it, as wide as it was deep and high—almost perfectly round in fact—with two glinting eyes notched in the front, a ruddy face with a small nose whose tip seemed faintly but perpetually blistered by the sun, and a crown of receding golden hair.

It's unlikely that any contemporary narrative could break into such a brutal head and truly evoke its workings. Sheridan's righteousness for all that his people had achieved and his rage at weakness were as evident as murder. While Nolan lived in a place inaccessible to him, beyond the generational divide, already fathoming tools to live in the future, Sheridan fingered the watch fob, his eyes narrowed. Yes, he'd done well in business, owning two general stores and the state's only paper mill, but raising a family had been a trial. He couldn't imagine an America without a Sheridan to fight its wars and drive fear into its oppressed peoples. He speculated that since Nolan's mother's womb had been faulty and produced only a single child, it must not have nourished the boy sufficiently. And then, to make matters worse, she'd kept him on apron strings.

Studying Nolan, he calculated the likelihood of his seed surviving, the way a farmer might stare at a field on the morning after an early frost.

———

One, two, three years passed during which the great challenges of Nolan's life were dressing, eating, defecating, and making his way back to bed. The effort of self-control burned away fat and muscle. He walked in a jittery, skeletal dance, his arms like corkscrews. His tongue was a knot, and each mental short circuit translated into his hand beating time on his thigh, his leg pumping. The slightest sound was unbearable: a car horn, the tooting of a far-off train. Startled, his body writhed like a snake on a pitchfork.

But in his childhood bed, during the slow convalescence, silence overwhelmed him. He lived with hardly more than the occasional word to the maid, the daughter of a formerly enslaved man from Georgia. She kept the house and cooked with such silence that she appeared stealthy, though she was just terrified of her employer. If Nolan's mother were still alive, he could have spoken to her, but though he missed her, he'd taken her portrait from his wall and placed it face down on the dresser, limiting his contact with the dead.

On occasion, he took Joseph's violin from the leather bag. It was nothing special: nicked and dented, worn to wood at the edges, a dark gold hue where the varnish was thickest. From inside its vents, its odor was so rich and improbable—dust, ocean brine, engine oil, wood smoke—that it must have been the result of decades of travel and not the perfume of a single home.

The bag also contained worn clothes that smelled of the trenches, and a note:

*Je n'ai jamais aimé les histoires. Je m'excuse, Félicité. Je t'ai aimée. Je t'aime toujours. Je t'ai trahie par amour. Je t'ai abandonnée pour te protéger.*

He recognized only *Je t'ai aimée.* It was some form of what he'd told the French prostitute before her wall had fallen down. Beneath the note were written the words: *Poster à Félicité Dubé, fille d'Albert Dubé, Rivière-au-Renard, Québec.*

He took the paper, made his way to the door, and eased down on the handle. He cleared the latch noiselessly and looked out: hallway empty. The study was on the second floor, near Nolan's room. He went in among the leather seats and shelves and drew back on the curtains. Among tomes of the frontier and white men forging a continent for their God, he found the old French-English dictionary.

Sweat beaded on his forehead as his fingers struggled for purchase on the fluttering edges of the pages. The precision of the task ignited a headache at the base of his skull. The memory of Joseph's sad life hovered about him, like the tones of his song.

Nolan worked a little each day, keeping the note inside the dictionary, translating a few words at a time. Eventually, he made sense of the first line: *I never liked stories.*

"Nolan!" It was his father. Nolan's hands shook as he went to the door and let himself into the hallway. His father was ascending the stairs.

"Nolan," he said, his voice almost casual, as if they talked this way daily. "I've spoken to Sheriff McCullough. He has a position that's just right for you, for how you are these days, though I'm sure you'll outgrow it when you're better."

"P-p-position?" Nolan said.

"Indeed, you'll be doing a little back-office clerking—no policing, that's for sure. Responsibilities will do you good. A few days of work, and you'll be a changed man."

After Nolan dressed properly, they went outside. His arms and legs wanted to go in every direction, but he herded them forward. The courthouse jail was an interminable ten blocks away.

There, Sheriff McCullough explained that the job required little more than sitting at a desk, tallying prisoners and, when a new one arrived, asking his age, address, and occupation. The deputies and courthouse clerks kept glancing over between tasks, chuckling and giving each other knowing looks.

"This will be your desk," his father told him, speaking to Nolan as if he were a child. "Why don't you try staying here until you finish work?"

He and the sheriff watched as Nolan sat down.

"Attaboy," the sheriff said, and they turned and left.

Though Nolan's hands trembled on the wood, something in his throat and chest felt locked, frozen with the animal terror of a creature about to die. He avoided looking around the courthouse. He stared out the second-floor window, pinning his gaze on the street, on the storefronts and signs, their wood and brick and printed glass.

The ticking of the clock grew louder. He closed his eyes—letting the war gather in his head. He opened them, seeing the street again, picturing it all released in a flash, dissolved in flame. But nothing happened, and eventually he returned home.

Nearing his house, he passed a young woman with strawberry hair and freckles.

"You're Sarah, aren't you?" he said, not stuttering. "Sarah Jenkins." He knew her from high school.

"Yes," she almost whispered, "and you're Nolan."

"That's right."

She blushed faintly, the freckles on her pale arms becoming dark.

"How have you been?" he asked, preserving this sudden, inexplicable ease.

"Oh, okay."

Her eyes darted to and from his face. She looked as if she'd been in a hurry, but his steadiness perfected the moment. Maybe her touch would cure him.

"I'm sorry. I have to run an errand," she said. He realized he'd been staring and smiling, nodding faintly.

"Okay, well, have a good day," he told her and smiled some more.

He watched her leave before he made his way to his house.

That night, in bed, he held his cock, picturing Sarah. As she took off her dress, she became the French girl in the moment he told her that he loved her. She was looking at him in surprise, not as if he'd said something foolish but had revealed himself to be human. He focused past this, on her breasts, and tried to master his hand.

It had been a long time since he'd sensed the edge of this feeling. But as it grew, so too did the whistling, so distantly at first that he failed to notice it until it emanated from deep inside his skull. He stopped and clutched himself, unable to continue for fear that the fire he'd escaped in France might burst from his head.

The jail job marked a turning point. His father was right. Soon he crossed streets, resisting the evocations of his mind. The war became like something in a room that he avoided looking at: an open fly, a tomato seed on a tie, a crosswise glimpse of a woman's cleavage, except that what he saw wasn't embarrassing or harmless or titillating.

Each day, he trekked the ten blocks to work hoping to see Sarah Jenkins, and when he did pass a young woman, his feet fell into line. At the jail, he recorded the number of prisoners—usually a drifter or two, or a black youth—and when a new one was brought in, he stammered the usual questions: name, address, and occupation.

Often, the prisoners resembled his visions of the dead. They sat, heads bowed, outlined in the faint emanation of the barred window, or, as he passed, their spectral faces lifted. He saw such men in his bathroom, examining their gory hands, or on the sidewalk. He always glanced at the feet of passersby to know who was living, since the dead did not move their feet.

Nor could the dead ring doorbells, and for this reason, when— shortly after Nolan had returned home for lunch—a strange colored man arrived, Nolan accepted that he was living. Besides, the dead were usually men he'd known.

"You should g-g-go around to the s-side d-door, b-b-boy," Nolan told him.

"Pardon me," the man said, his accent distinctly Eastern. He wore a fine gray suit and held to his chest a matching hat.

"It's for c-c-coloreds," Nolan told him.

"But I'm Indian."

"Ind-d-dian?"

The man's cheekbones bulged like eggs beneath his dark skin, and his straight black hair was parted, brushed to the side. No Indian had ever come to the door, and Nolan didn't know the rule for them. Besides, the man's suit was clearly expensive.

"W-what do you n-n-need?"

"I am looking to speak with a Mr. Myron Sheridan. I'm doing research for Harvard University in Cambridge, Massachusetts—"

"H-Harvard has Indians?"

"Harvard has had Indian graduates for over two hundred years. I am conducting research on the Wounded Knee Battle of 1890. Mr. Sheridan received a Medal of Honor for his service there."

"He's my f-f-f-father."

"Excellent. I have been interviewing the survivors of the battle, and your father's contribution would be invaluable."

Nolan gave a panicked nod. The Indian was crazy, to come and knock on a white man's door, wanting to question him. But he was well spoken and well dressed, and that was intimidating. Since Nolan had taken the jail job, his father had been around less and less, and he was out now. Nolan said so. The Indian removed a card from his pocket and wrote on the back the address of a hotel in the Greenwood district, for colored. In typeface, on the front, were the words, *Henry Clay — Harvard University.*

The Indian left, and Nolan went inside. He sat on a couch and gave himself over to twitching. His own failures had never been clearer than when he stood before the educated Indian.

———

Since taking the job at the jail, Nolan ceased having dinner alone and joined his father. That night, their forks and knives scratched at their plates, their chewing loud. He intended to mention Henry Clay, but he considered that once he told his father, the matter would be out of his own hands. He would likely learn nothing about why a strange Harvard Indian had come to the door and asked about a battle Nolan had never heard of.

After dinner, instead of sitting with the French-English dictionary and working on the translation (he'd recently deciphered the second line—*I am sorry, Félicité*), he left the house and made his way into Greenwood.

The sun was low, the May sky carpeted in mauve, gusty and warm, and the day's heat diminishing fast. It was late to be calling on anyone, much less an Indian in a colored hotel, and word could get around. He hesitated and then went inside and asked the young desk clerk if a Mr. Henry Clay was in.

"Just one moment, sir."

The clerk climbed the stairs and knocked on a door.

Like boxcars on the long track of speech, words began to cram together in Nolan's head. Sweat dampened his back.

The young man returned to his desk, and Henry Clay came down, smoothing his gray suit. His hair was not quite so well managed, dark strands on his high forehead.

"You are Mr. Sheridan's son, I believe."

"That's r-r-right," Nolan told him. "I c-c-came to ask a few questions and set up a m-m-meeting with my f-f-father."

"I see," Henry said. "What questions would you like to ask?"

"Well, f-f-for instance, p-p-perhaps—perhaps you can explain what sorts of information you would l-l-like from my f-f-father concerning—concerning—"

"Wounded Knee?"

"Yes."

"We are trying to create a more complete account. I would simply like to transcribe his memories for the Harvard archives."

Nolan shook his head as if to get water from his ears.

"S-so the battle was important because of the mmm-mm-medals?"

"It is the battle for which the most American soldiers received Medals of Honor. In fact, your father was one of twenty."

Behind the counter, the young clerk kept his gaze lowered, as if reading, though he appeared alert enough. A white man discussing family history with an Indian in a hotel for coloreds would be grade-A gossip.

"I d-d-don't know much about history," Nolan said. "I n-n-never really even understood why we had to go to F-F-France."

Henry appeared patient enough, though he nodded curtly each time Nolan finished a difficult word.

"I could explain that if you would like."

Nolan flushed. "That's all right. But mmmm-maybe I can speak f-f-frankly."

He'd lowered his voice, and it seemed that the clerk leaned forward a bit.

"Shall we sit?" Henry said. He motioned Nolan toward a couch in an alcove.

The springs creaked beneath them as they took their places.

"You were saying?"

"I'd like to speak f-f-frankly. I've never known much about my f-f-father's service. He's p-proud, and he doesn't brag. I'd be greatly indebted by what you could tell me. I'd do all I can to secure an interview for you."

Henry narrowed his eyes and nodded to himself.

"Wounded Knee," he said, "was a significant battle against the Sioux Indians in South Dakota. The circumstances were complex. There was a religious revival at that time called the Ghost Dance, a form of circular sun dance. It originated in Nevada, among the Paviotso Indians, and . . ."

Spine straight, palms on his knees, Nolan sat, managing to nod now and then, the motion more sudden than he intended. Normally his mind was as distracted as his body, but he followed Henry's explanation of a prophet Wodziwob who had taught the dance that was reintroduced twenty years later by a young Paiute named Wovoka. During a solar eclipse, Wovoka had a fever and a vision—"What modern medical science recognizes as delirium," Henry said. "Wovoka claimed that through the dance the world would be renewed. All men, white and Indian, would live in peace, and the dead and living would be reunited."

Henry's words startled Nolan. For reasons he couldn't explain, the thought of Indians dancing to heal themselves made him think of Joseph's song, of that one moment he'd been free from the blasted, cratered front.

"So the dance actually h-healed them?"

"Unfortunately, no. When the Sioux learned it, they were desperate and suffering greatly. Their way of life had been destroyed, and the buffalo were gone. They performed the dance to restore the world and eliminate the white men. They danced so that their dead comrades would return, as would the prairie grasses and the buffalo."

"And this dance . . . ," Nolan said, speaking easily enough now, the muscles of his jaw increasingly obedient, "what did it have to do with the b-b-battle?"

"Well, imagine hundreds of Indians dancing for the destruction of the white man."

Nolan couldn't think of what else to say. He needed time to consider this.

"I will talk to my f-f-father about your interest, but he's out of town at the moment," he lied. "Can I get back to you t-t-tomorrow?"

---

In the morning, a black teenager was brought into the jail. He'd been accused of grabbing a seventeen-year-old white girl in an elevator. The sheriff questioned him. The boy insisted he'd tripped and reached for her arm.

"So why were you hiding?" the sheriff asked, squinting, his eyes in a pleat.

"I w-w-was afraid," the boy stammered.

The sheriff nodded. It was self-evident. No sane black man wouldn't be afraid. They took him up to the jail, and the sheriff told Nolan to fill out the boy's form.

"Is it b-b-bad?" Nolan asked.

"I'll not have a lynching like last year. That's all I got to say."

Nolan tapped his thigh.

"You pray to Jesus," the sheriff said, putting his hand on Nolan's shoulder. "He just might fix that for you."

Nolan took the clipboard and made his way to the cells.

The boy was sitting but lifted his damp face from his hands. He was maybe three years younger than Nolan, but solidly built.

Nolan positioned the pen.

"N-name?" he asked.

"W-w-what the heck you f-f-fraid of? I'm the one b-behind bars."

"N-n-name?" Nolan repeated, wondering if it was fear that shredded the nerves.

"Rowland," the young man said. "I d-d-didn't do nothing you know."

"I just n-n-need to enter your inf-f-formation."

"They c-call me Dick Rowland."

"Occup-p-p-pation?"

The boy sighed and closed his eyes.

"I'm a shoeshine boy."

*Shoeshine*, Nolan wrote and then asked, "Address?"

Rowland was staring off. His bottom lip had begun to quiver again.

"I didn't do n-nothing," he said. "What kind of idiot would grab a white girl?"

Nolan couldn't stand it. He got a tin cup of water for himself and a second one that he set inside the bars, on the floor. He returned to the desk, to his usual position at the window, trying to keep the street from combusting in his brain.

After work, when Nolan arrived at Henry's hotel, the young desk clerk hurried upstairs.

Henry appeared to have been napping and to have dressed in a hurry.

"Is your father back already?"

"No," Nolan said. "I thought . . ."

He motioned to the couch.

Henry glanced over as if it would be the subject of their conversation.

"I have mmm-more questions," Nolan told him.

Henry's eyes went cold, their lids lowering.

"I see. Well. Fine, then. Let's sit."

Nolan joined him, his back like a ramrod. He inhaled.

"Do you know the dance?"

Henry frowned. "I'm afraid not. My interest is in Wounded Knee. But let me get the study by James Mooney. He compiled it for the government and describes both the Ghost Dance and the massacre."

When Henry returned with his leather-bound tome, Nolan said, "Mm-massacre?"

"Ah, yes, slip of the tongue. Some people do call it that."

He rapidly opened the book.

"Does it talk about the massacre?" Nolan asked.

"Yes, but you wanted to know about the Ghost Dance?"

"I do, but what does it say about the massacre?"

Henry sighed. He explained that Wounded Knee was a confrontation between about five hundred US cavalry and a hundred Sioux warriors camped with over two hundred women and children. He cleared his throat and read.

"At the first volley the Hotchkiss guns that were trained on the camp opened fire and sent a storm of shells and bullets among the women and children, who had gathered in front of the teepees to watch the unusual spectacle of military display. The guns poured in two-pound explosive shells at the rate of nearly fifty per minute, mowing down everyone—"

"You came," Nolan interrupted, "to interview my father about that?"

Henry paused, his hands trembling slightly.

"I should have explained the situation better. You see, it's hard to know for sure how it all happened. Some soldiers went to take away the Indians' guns, and—"

"What do you want to know from him?"

"We're just hoping to record the event more thoroughly."

As a child, Nolan had coveted the Medal of Honor bestowed on his father by the president himself. He would ask to look at it in its bureau drawer, its image of Minerva lifting a shield to fend off Discord and his serpents.

"Pardon me for saying this," Henry said, "but have you even mentioned my presence to your father? I didn't come here to deliver lessons on history."

"But the Ghost Dance?" Nolan asked. "You never saw it?"

"I'm afraid not, but the records indicate that the Indians shuffled about in a circle, well beyond the point of exhaustion. There were many chants to accompany the dance. The Arapaho sang, 'My Father, have pity on me! I have nothing to eat. I am dying of thirst. Everything is gone!' The traditional chant was '*kosi' wûmbi'ndomä*'—'There is dust from the whirlwind.'"

"And you are sure that nobody was healed?"

Henry began to stand but hesitated.

"There are theories that the dance was a sort of hypnosis in which dancers made peace with the dead. Some inquiring white men learned the dance and claimed that it cured them of their ailments. There is record of this."

He got up from the couch and made a slight bow.

"When your father is back, please come again. I bid you goodnight."

———

Each autumn when Nolan was a child, after the crickets burrowed into the earth, he sensed his mother's frustration with the house's silence. She loved to garden and once told him he'd grown in her like a seed. At a fair, she paid an old man who dipped a needle in India ink to write his name, Nolan Myron Sheridan, on a corn kernel that she helped him plant in the garden and from which they later harvested six ears of corn.

His father showed no interest in nature. He once mentioned native prairie grass he'd seen as a young man in the Seventh Cavalry, the rare extravagant grasses so tall that only on horseback could he view the horizon. But he preferred no talk at all. Nolan grew up fearing his father's moods, the way opening a door startled him and elicited his rage. His father yelled at him for sneaking up when Nolan was simply entering a room.

Now Nolan lay in bed as the drapes gathered moonlight. He got up and pulled them back, releasing the glow into the room. He opened the window, and feeling the cool, steady night breeze he could imagine the distance it had traveled. Against his skin, it was a continuation of the plains.

Standing in the middle of the room, he pictured himself alone on the prairies, lifting his face to the sun. From the warmth against his skin, he would know the world could change—not burned up but renewed: French villages reassembling from exploded stone; the bits of obliterated soldiers gliding like mercury, finding old forms and returning across the ocean to those they loved.

He pushed his feet in short steps. He struggled to breathe as the shadows about him became men. Tanks scrabbled like giant lice. Artillery flashed on the horizon—distant, frenetic lightning. Shells shrieked and roared. Miles of barbed wire sang when struck. Then the whistling began, the feeling of helplessness.

His foot twisted, and he threw out his hand, swiping the face-down picture frame from the top of the dresser. Glass shattered. His mother's luminous face looked up at him solemnly, as if she'd been interred in the floor.

Down the hall, his father's door handle rattled. Footsteps approached and paused just outside.

Nolan stood, pale as ice in moonlit pajamas, his lungs struggling like an animal in a box.

The floor creaked and the footsteps receded. At the end of the hall, the handle clacked and the latch snapped into place.

———

A dozen deputies arrived at the jail, armed with rifles and shotguns. They passed around the afternoon edition of the *Tribune*, huddling to read two articles encouraging the lynching, all the while debating among themselves whether they should be defending the boy and not outside with the folks demanding justice.

A little later, Sheriff McCullough hurried in.

"Nolan," he said. "Head on home. Some business done come up you don't want to be around for."

The deputies chuckled as they watched him go. He stood on the sidewalk, panting as if the air in his lungs were shame and he had to get it out.

A crowd had gathered, cars pulling up, men looking at the courthouse, squinting in the afternoon light.

As Nolan neared home, a breeze blew in from the river. A crow cawed in the pines next to the house. He was climbing his front steps when a young woman came to the screen door just inside.

She stopped, her red hair in a loose braid on her shoulder and the screen shadowing her face as if she wore a mourning veil.

"Sarah?" he said.

She pushed open the door and stepped outside. The late afternoon sun against the house had turned the windows to amber and lit golden shards in the green of her eyes.

"Did you come by to say hello?" Nolan asked.

She held her hands clasped at her waist and looked off into the distance.

"I . . ."

"Are you okay?"

"I'm all right. It's just that . . . I never told you. My folks passed away from the influenza after the war. I was sick myself, but your father says I have a good constitution."

She blushed and looked down as if to indicate her constitution, and he followed her gaze. Her freckles darkened, as distinctly patterned as the markings on a trout.

Nolan's father came to the door.

"You're home early," he said. He was tucking in his shirttails, his suspenders down.

A muscle throbbed in Nolan's throat.

"Something's g-g-going on at the courthouse," he finally said.

His father looked Sarah over.

"You can head on home now, Sarah."

"Thank you, Mr. Sheridan."

Nolan glanced after her, but his father motioned him inside. He started up the stairs. Nolan just stood there. He understood why his father had gotten him the job.

"Ma died only a few years ago," he said.

His father stopped. He spoke without even turning.

"I'm sorry, boy. But I can't rely on you to pass on the family name."

*Je n'ai jamais aimé les histoires.* "I never liked stories."

*Je m'excuse, Félicité.* "I am sorry, Félicité."

*Je t'ai aimée.* "I loved you."

*Je t'aime toujours.* "I still love you."

*Je t'ai trahie par amour.* "I betrayed you out of love."

*Je t'ai abandonnée pour te protéger.* "I abandoned you to protect you."

And below: "Mail to Félicité Dubé, daughter of Albert Dubé . . ."

Nolan returned to his bedroom and undressed for bed. He hesitated and approached the mirror. He did so carefully, from the side, making sure no dead hung about in its depths. The dusty glass showed a starched white face. His chest was a washboard, with the small pink nipples of a child. His limbs were long and pale, like bones uniformed in skin.

He dressed again and eased open the door. He crept along the hall and down the stairs, commanding his body to obedience.

He paused on the vantage of his porch. The moon shone along the river, but toward the courthouse, floodlights overwhelmed its glow. Shouts and laughter carried in the dark.

His hand began to tap his thigh as he hurried. On disobedient feet, he made his way into the Greenwood district.

At the hotel, the clerk was still at his desk, reading. He rubbed his eyes.

"Looking for Mr. Clay?"

When Henry descended the stairs, he did so slowly, his face not that of a man woken from sleep, but of one disturbed in his work.

"Yes, Mr. Sheridan?"

"I want you to teach me."

"Teach you what?"

"The dance."

Henry glanced at the young clerk who looked away, scratching suddenly at the back of his head.

"I'm sorry, Mr. Sheridan, I cannot do that."

Henry turned and climbed the stairs again. Nolan called after him, but Henry didn't pause. From the second floor came the sound of a door closing.

The clerk didn't look up. Nolan flushed and went outside. Eventually, he came to a small park. He placed his hat on a bench and sat and unlaced his shoes. He removed them and set them side by side. He carefully rolled his socks off, turned them right-side out, folded them, and placed them on the shoes. Then he stepped onto the park green. A few youths running past stopped to stare.

The earth scraped against Nolan's feet as he tried to relax into the movements. The spasms in his legs diminished, his arms swung at his sides, but beneath the motion, his body still trembled, tension locked in his chest. And then, gradually, as he shuffled in a circle, the tension shifted, moving like heat along his spine, into his throat. It boiled in his skull and released with a flash, filling the night.

The youths ran away as men cried out. A motor roared. Shots echoed. Smoke drifted past. Feeling as if a bone had snapped deep inside his body, he fell into a rhythm. His ribs expanded.

Bosch machine guns rattled like typewriters on the salient. Sirens wailed. Glass shattered. Soldiers charged, struggling in trenches, stepping on and over each other, slipping to their knees and still fighting.

A fire lit the sky like the dawn, and there were more sirens and gunshots. The real dawn came, paler, wary of the earth's conflagrations. A whistle blew, and the voices of men rose in a long, disjointed howl. Airplanes buzzed like hornets from which dark shapes fell and bloomed into fire.

Dead men stepped through the park's trees and passed Nolan, ignoring him. He was still dancing. Flames released into the sky as he shuffled past decimated blocks and trenches dug into the streets. Dim figures drew close again and again, studied him, and left.

———

I can't really say what dance Nolan intuited, invented, or appropriated in that little city park, or as he left Tulsa and followed the railroad tracks into the plains, until, strangely, he came upon two wounded men on the ground. Just as he had imagined the past in order to create the art of his own deliverance, I envisioned the scene he witnessed so that I could compose "Peacetime." I sang it in bars, strumming my guitar.

> *West for the prophet, he walks the tracks.*
> *On a shining hill, two men lie on their backs.*
> *The white fellow's dead, the Mexican bleeds.*
> *A hundred typed pages flutter in the weeds.*
>
> *Brambles, bushes, between the men is a book.*
> *A shard of moon hangs, daybreak is bright.*
> *The river curves like a lack of direction.*
> *He dances, dances for the resurrection.*
>
> *Broken by war, broken by men,*
> *He can't walk, he dances from sin.*
> *The city burns, the firebombs fall,*
> *But this was peace, so we forget it all.*

— II —

Silence. Father hates noise. He speaks with reverence of the quiet up here. Even the afternoon thunder, as it pounds across the mountain in slow, giant steps, sounds faint. The air is too thin to sustain the reverberations. Pine and aspen soften the wind.

First memories. Mother soothed me. She held me when I felt wild or sad, when emotion made me want to shout just to hear my voice. Sometimes, I wandered into the hills, challenging my fear of bears and wildcats, so that I could stand and cry out and listen to my voice dissolve in the atmosphere.

The violin was Father's concession to silence. Mama took me to town three times a week for lessons. She made me practice, in the hours when father collected wood and got water from the stream, when sunlight turned from long and golden between the trees to clumped purple above the mountains. She hired as my teacher an Irish miner whose leg had been crushed. He taught me camp songs and traditional reels. I also got lessons from a gypsy who played the violin on his knee, though Mama quickly called an end to that.

She settled on a man with an ageless face, a little like Father's. He played for money in the camps. He taught me well, resting his hand on my knee—to steady me, he said. He sometimes put it on my shoulder or back or thigh. When I told Mama, she would have none of it.

"He's a good teacher," she said. "One should look not at a man's flaws but at his strengths."

Father resembles a boy but for his height and white hair.

One night, when I was eight, I woke. I turned in my blankets. I saw that only Mama was in her bed. Moonlight in the windows reminded me of winter. I shivered and burrowed deeper. The dark lines between the floorboards made me think of an accordion played in town by an old man with a curly silver mane. As clouds moved along the moon, the boards expanded and retracted, the earth slowly breathing beneath us.

Father had been in the outhouse a long time. The clouds passed and returned. Moonlight ebbed against the glass.

I slipped my legs from beneath the sheets. Between each step, I paused to listen. Air blew along the door's edges. I leaned my shoulder into it, pinning it in place to release the tension from the latch. I lifted it, stepped out, and lowered the latch.

The path threaded through the trees, along a rise to the out-house. I hurried in the cool air, the earth almost warm beneath my feet. I stopped. A faint scuffing sound reached me, like the panting of a dog. It was steady, rhythmic. I turned to run and get Mama. I'd seen her strike a bear with the broom as it came up the stairs. She put the bristles into its eyes, and it scrambled back and ran.

But the wind died, and I listened again. The sound wasn't an animal's breath. Something was being rubbed, like the sanding of a board.

I took a few steps toward it. Mama once said I'd inherited the disposition of her father's people—the lack of fear or respect for the law. She'd also told me she would instill it in me with a strap. I moved through the shadowed forest. The rubbing got louder, a foot scuffing the earth.

I stood a long time as my father moved in the moonlit clearing, in a rhythmic, circular shuffle. He swung his arms. His head lolled from side to side. Suddenly, his motions became more fluid, the way a horse, after its first few steps, finds a rolling gait. Sometimes he threw his arms up as if to protect himself. He groaned or mut-tered. The shuffling didn't pause.

I watched until I was almost falling asleep against the tree. The tang of pine floated about my face, the coarse bark beneath my hand. As a faint silver line appeared along the mountains, I with-drew through the shadows and returned to my bed. I heard Father come in not long after. His mattress creaked. Through cracked eyes, I saw Mama turn and pull his head to her chest. She moved her fingers through his hair. From his breathing, I could tell he was asleep.

When I was ten, my father stopped working at the general store. I didn't know why. We suddenly had new mattresses and new windows and whatever Mama wanted in the kitchen, which wasn't much. I understood we had money now, but we lived almost the same. All of us slept in our cabin's single room. Moonlight came through the glass a little more clearly, a luxury of the rich.

That was also when he left for the first time. He was gone two or three weeks. Mama cut wood and brought in water. She got groceries in town. During his absence, she stopped speaking to me in those other words, the ones only she and I understood.

"So you can be an American," she said.

"Why wouldn't I be an American?" I asked in the words I was no longer allowed to speak.

"What? I don't understand."

"Why wouldn't I be an American?" I said the way she wanted me to.

"You are an American."

"But why wouldn't I be one if I said it like this." And I said it again, the way I had before.

"Because that's not how Americans speak."

I just nodded. And so I stopped. The memory of understanding those words would remain, but with time I no longer recalled them clearly. I was sure that if someone spoke them to me, the words would return to my mouth as easy as breathing. But no one spoke them.

"Where has Father gone?" I asked.

She hesitated.

"He is gone to see some things."

That's all she said of his absence until three years later, on the third time he went away, again in July, again for several weeks. She was standing over the stove.

In response to my question, she said, "It is a pilgrimage."

"Father's a pilgrim?"

"In his way."

And so I waited another year. I almost forgot. I wasn't quite fourteen, and new, more vital thoughts were on my mind. I played the violin daily. I did my school work. This was 1959, and I'd come to realize how poor I looked to the other kids, with my mended clothes, my one-room cabin in the mountains. We had money, but neither Mama nor Father had any desire to live like the people in town. I'm not sure they even noticed the difference. Other boys had their own rooms. They played guitar and snuck off to smoke together or crept through girls' windows at night. Each morning I had to lie in bed motionless, pretending to be asleep so that my erection could deflate. I pictured Mama plucking and gutting a chicken. That usually helped to speed the softening.

July arrived. Father talked to me about taking a job in town, how that would build character. But I told him that the violin would be my career and that I wanted to apply to a conservatory in the east. He studied me with his green, watery eyes. His gaunt boy's face was inexpressive, always slightly dazed, as if he'd just woken up. He nodded once.

I played everywhere, on the hills around the house, on stumps in the forest or rocks overlooking the valley and the town. I worried that the music would bother Father. He'd nailed a layer of cloth around the edge of the door so it couldn't slam. He touched everything with the same cautiousness that men employ when approaching snakes. He took cups from the kitchen board slowly and gingerly. Even his way of splitting wood was silent, the axe accurate, his lean body exerting only the exact force necessary. But I think the constant music habituated him in some way. He appeared less cautious, more relaxed, moving more easily across the yard, up the stairs, and into the house.

When he left this time, I almost didn't see him go. It was before dawn. I was curled in bed, my hands between my legs, nursing my aching erection, squeezing it gently but firmly, the way I might a wasp sting. The front door whispered closed. He was so precise in his rituals that I knew this wasn't the hour for his circular dance. The wrong shade of silver encroached against the dark over the July mountains.

I dressed silently, praying mother wouldn't wake. My embarrassment was still at half-mast as I stripped off my flannels and pulled on my pants. I took a few coins from the bowl under the sink, behind the tea cloth.

I followed him at a distance, waiting at curves in the road. He didn't go into town but turned south or east at each fork. His lank figure seemed to move only beneath the knees, his torso motionless, as if he were still sleeping as he stepped along the roadside.

When he stopped at a store to buy a snack, I waited in the trees. I stopped at the same store after he left. The mountains became more gently sloping. A railroad track ran through them, winding between low passes. His figure diminished. It climbed onto the station platform. Hours later, the train rumbled into the valley. He boarded and was gone.

When I got home, it was night. Mama stood on the porch, flushed, her hands open at her sides and her fingers slightly curled, as if she might ball them into fists. She spoke in that old language. She was telling me to come inside. I do not remember the words.

Over the next two years, each July, Father made his usual pilgrimage, and I didn't follow. I was months from my sixteenth birthday when I tried again. I'd grown. I'd taken over chopping wood and played violin in the new restaurants near the ski resort. Girls a few years older than me snuck out to meet me. They were visitors, here with their families from Denver or faraway places: California, the East Coast.

So I walked up to the platform. The money I had was my own, earned from music. I was as tall as Father, broader through the chest, which doesn't say much. I had Mama's black hair and his eyes, but I didn't know where I'd gotten my muscles and size. I stood next to him, my hands in my pockets.

"I'm coming with you."

He just nodded in that staccato way. We boarded the train and found our seats and were soon rushing east. The mountains fell away, and the land was flat but for a few homesteads and windmills, the horizon as long and bright as a knife. I had a sense of ritual: the landscape an altar before a flat yellow infinity.

We traveled through the night and the following day, changing trains twice. We got off in Tulsa and walked the streets, until we were on a residential lane.

"Go slow now," he told me. "Keep your head down. Look casual."

The houses here were older than any I'd seen before, larger, not efficient in their shapes like those in our town, but proud, colorfully shingled, rambling upon their properties and surrounded by trees and flowering hedges. With dusk, the darkening bulk of the eastern horizon lifted the plate of the sky, tilting it slowly above our heads.

Father almost stopped as he passed before a house. Through a large window, a family of three was having Sunday dinner. They were well dressed. The old man I might have taken for a grandfather but for the strength of his carriage, the way he cut the meat and glanced to speak to the young man across from him. The woman—pale and freckled, with graying red hair—drew my attention less than her son.

He looked a little older than me. There was something stern in his face. He had sandy blond hair and a jaw like Father's, but Father's head appeared as if it had been worn thin after centuries in a riverbed. This youth head's was neither strong nor weak. I couldn't find the word for his head. What was it? Indifferent almost.

Only when Father and I had moved on, walking along the street, did the word come to me. Dutiful. He had a dutiful head.

We passed in front of the house several more times. Father said nothing. I knew by the third loop that the old man was his father, my grandfather. The woman was not one of us. The young man was my half-uncle.

———

"It's hard to make sense of it all. Just pieces. Sometimes I feel I was blown apart in the war and put together from the bodies of different men. The parts never wanted to work together, but I had all these pieces. Pieces of a body. Pieces of stories."

Father didn't begin talking until we'd left the train. Over the course of the day that we walked home through the mountains, he spoke—formally, carefully, as if he'd been planning this story for years, or reading from a book. Each hour, he said more words than he had in all the years of my life. By the time I reached my porch, I had a history.

"I was born a Sheridan, but it's not a name I chose to keep. It's not a name I could be proud of. I was raised to believe we were warriors. We'd conquered the plains. We were a greater race spreading civilization. That's how my father spoke. I went to war unafraid because I hadn't been taught to be afraid. I believed I would find the element for which I was destined. It broke me. I was hardly in it before it broke me. And it saved me. It stripped me of myth."

We walked along the contours of mountains, the sun hot and the shadows of trees so dark across the road they resembled gullies. I saw the young man's face again. Duty. Father had been like this once as well.

"The night before my first battle, I met your grandfather— your mother's father, the man for whom you are named. He was playing a violin on the front. I was sitting in a hole I dug, but he stood there exposed, facing the German lines. He was older than the rest of us, strong looking, but I'd hardly noticed him. He was there without quite being there. The rest of us were young and bouncing off the world, and he might as well have been a tree he was so much a part of this earth. I looked over and saw him stand up and put the violin to his chin. A few of the Germans took shots, but others shouted not to. The nights were long on the front. No one wanted to kill the music.

"After he played, I joined him in his hole. It was almost dawn. He looked exhausted. We all were, but I saw something in his face then. He wouldn't have been bothered if the bullets had hit him. The only thing that mattered was that violin and the song. My father used to whistle it to himself. It was an old Irish melody. If I hadn't recognized it, I'm not sure I would have spoken to him. And if I hadn't, you wouldn't be here today.

"He told me a story. I knew from the way he spoke he was a man who never talked. It was a deathbed confession. He was ready to end his story. I don't think he could have dreamed he was starting a new one."

Father described the war and the shell that incinerated his nerves. I pictured pine branches on a campfire, the crackling needles. He told me about the violin, the note in French, and returning home in shame, as well as about Henry Clay and the burning of Tulsa's black district, how—seeing planes left over from the First

World War dropping firebombs on homes and businesses—he'd believed the war had burst from his head.

"That was June 1921. I wouldn't meet your mother until 1940. I had a vague idea about finding the prophet of the Ghost Dance, out in Nevada. But as I walked the railroad track, I came across two men lying on the ground. The white man was dead, but the Mexican was only wounded. After your grandfather and Henry Clay, he was the next man to give me part of our story. I guess I was trying to create one that I could live with from whatever pieces I could find.

"A black family lived not too far away in an old stucco house they'd rebuilt. The father and his four sons lifted the Mexican. He was small, and carrying him didn't require much effort. They thought I was wounded, too, and tried to help me along. There was a book lying on the ground, next to the man. I took that with me. It wasn't in a language I could read.

"That night, I was sitting next to the wounded man. He was thin and dark, with hard lines in his face, but quite young, I realized as I studied him. The mother had put a wool blanket over my shoulders. I was empty inside. The war was gone for now. Its embers still burned, but there was space for a future.

"The Mexican stirred. I leaned close and, in his fevered state, he whispered, *Estrada*. I was so empty that I caught the name, the way a spiderweb catches a raindrop. I became Nolan Estrada, and as if I'd taken his burden, the Mexican lived. He spoke no English. One dawn, he could move again. He sat by the fire. He stared into the flames. He asked me something several times: *¿Está muerto?*

"One of the family's sons joined us. He told me his sweetheart was Mexican and he'd learned some Spanish. 'He's asking if the other man is dead,' he told me. I said yes, and he turned to the Mexican. '*Sí*,' he told him, and the Mexican lowered his head with such a look of grief and rage that I didn't know if the dead man was his enemy or closest friend. A few nights later, he was gone, though he left the book, whose author was also Estrada. The boy told me that the Mexican had departed to find the woman he loved. So if it's not yet clear to you, it soon will be: There's not much original about men.

"I wandered west then, toward Nevada, to find the prophet. But I found the mountains instead. I'd never been in such a contained landscape or so close to the sky. Something in me calmed. I didn't intend to stay, but the sign on the town's general store said it was looking for a clerk. I took the job. Mining kept the economy strong then, but I wasn't fit for the mines. After ten years, I began returning to Tulsa. I never spoke to my father again. I never will. But once a year, I walked past the house so I could see him with his new sons. The family grew. Three, four sons, a daughter, a second daughter, and finally another son—the one you saw. Then, fifteen years later, I met the Mexican on the road. I wouldn't have recognized him, but he knew me instantly. He spoke English by then."

Silently now, Father walked on, his feet gliding over the earth, his carriage stiff and his shoulders motionless. The rising road wound along a deep valley. The air was growing thin and familiar.

"It's hard to know how to say this," Father told me. "I hadn't known a woman. I was getting on toward forty when I met the Mexican again. I'd found a life of solitude here in Colorado, and though I worked, I wasn't a man women would approach. But the Mexican told me his story. He told me he'd met a woman soldier during the revolution, and he'd slowly won her love with the book. He told me that after he'd been shot, after he'd healed, he'd returned to find her. In each border town, he heard stories of a young woman who'd been captured by the Mexican authorities that had been seeking him, since he was an outlaw for his writing, for speaking out against injustice. They caught her, but she escaped. And then she grew bitter. She believed he'd abandoned her and claimed his own freedom in America. One night the soldier she'd been, she became again. People recalled how different she looked. She killed the men who held her prisoner. The authorities tried to capture her. She traveled along the border. The stories people told were of lawmen who turned up dead, of bandits who wanted her for a bride. He knew these were stories. After years looking for her, or for her grave, he returned to America where the stories could not follow and he could forget. He said he hadn't given up, that there are always clues to the past.

"'Look,' he told me, 'we have crossed on this road, and I have recognized your face. You saved me. And maybe my words today, or my story, will save you too.'

"We made a small fire in a field of scrub brush and spoke all night. I told him about the French prostitute during the war. I described her small room, my irrefutable desire, her destitution, and how I hadn't cared. The shell had fallen and blown out the wall, and her rage showed how much she would grieve that lost space."

This conversation that Father described to me I would write over and over years later, trying to picture it accurately, to see these men as men and not ideas of a lost, mythical America. I was afraid that Rafael was less a person than a prophetic bearer of a message, a token figure, like Henry Clay or Dick Rowland, come to nuance the humanity of our family—to give us, by their inclusion in our story, further jurisdiction over America, allowing us to feel that we are more than brutal conquering white men, that our pain includes them, while our supremacy over this land steadily increases.

*'She must have suffered terribly,' Rafael said. 'She must have had nothing else.'*

*'Is it foolish to spend all these years thinking about a prostitute I never touched?'*

*'It's not foolish, unless everything we do is foolish.'*

*'I wanted to be touched. I didn't consider how it felt to be her, to be touched over and over so she could eat.'*

*'We are all loving something we have imagined.'*

*'She is all I have to remember. I will be old soon, and there is nothing else.'*

'*There is always something else if you open yourself to it.*'

'*Where did you find your wisdom?*'

'*In emptiness, in searching, in love I could not give another.*'

'*And the book you wrote, what is it about?*'

'*I did not write it. It wrote me.*'

Nolan considered the Ghost Dance then and admitted that he had stolen Rafael's name.

'*And I took it from another. Is any of us the first one to carry a name or anything that we call ours?*'

Nolan nodded, giving this some thought, considering that not all thefts are equal, that their weight is determined less by the object than by the person taking it.

'*You live in America now?*' he asked.

'*I have lived in several states. She must be searching for me in America.*'

'*Why here?*'

'*Because this is where I went.*'

'*And why would she have killed all of those people in Mexico?*'

'*Because they were the people who should have been killed or else a story of the justice people crave, but once they were dead, she would have looked somewhere else.*'

'*You only just realized that?*'

'*It took me twenty years. I gave up. I married. My wife died last year, and our twins joined the army. So I decided it was time to look again. The feeling of looking is an old one. It is a journey back to youth. I will find her this time. Her husband will be dead. She will run a hotel on the edge of a city. You can never find the people you love if you remember what they were. You must imagine who they will become. That was my mistake.*'

"Estrada's story seemed truly hopeless," Father told me. "I didn't give it much thought. But then, as I neared Tulsa—I was on my way there to observe the family for reasons I couldn't fully explain—I realized there were pieces of my history I hadn't resolved. I walked past the house as we did a few days ago. I saw my growing brothers, my father and stepmother—a girl I'd gone to high school with. Then I found a hotel room. I lay in my bed and thought it all through.

"That Sunday, while the family was at church, I went around to the back door. I lifted a brick on the footpath. The spare key was still imprinted in the gravel. The lock was the same. I went inside. Fifteen years, and a new family, and yet my father's will or stubbornness had preserved the place. The study had been turned into a bedroom for one of the boys, but I checked the shelves throughout the house. I found the old French-English dictionary on the living room bookshelf. It had become purely decorative, a pretty old book, but inside the back cover, there was the yellowed note your grandfather had written, so thin it had gone unnoticed. The violin was in one of the bedrooms, in its case, on a dresser. Someone had been playing it. I didn't care. Its history didn't belong here. No one in that house could have understood it.

"Then I went up to my father's room. I opened the drawer in his bureau. There was the medal he'd received from President Harrison—Minerva lifting a shield before Discord. I recalled the war, and my father's sudden rages, the way he jumped when someone came into a room quickly. His nerves had been burned up too. I was going to steal the medal and free the house of its curse. I didn't know yet that he would lose sons again in wars. Maybe if I'd walked out with that medal, they'd still be alive. But I kept hesitating. In the end, I couldn't take it. It was their history.

"So I found myself in Colorado with relics. A book I couldn't read. A violin I couldn't play. A letter that might reach no one. There was also the dance. The book had given me my name. The violin had given me my life. The dance had given me a new body and a new home, even if the dance was something I'd imagined and not learned from the prophet or his people. I'd seen so many broken bodies on a broken earth that I understood the wisdom in healing both together. So I just moved in a circle, feeling the earth with my feet. I don't know if I can call it a dance. It was a simple rhythmic movement—a painful shuffling to anyone who might have seen me—but with it, I understood how creating a space with your body can build you into someone new.

"And then there was the letter. It brought me a wife. I mailed it to Québec, and three years later, when I came into town to get my mail, a woman stood before the post office. She had the blackest hair I'd seen on a white person and blue, blue eyes. A widow. Her name was Riva. She spoke a little English, enough so that we could communicate. She was the daughter of the man who played the violin in France. She'd been conceived days before her parents' wedding. She didn't know why he'd abandoned them. I held the story of his life, it seemed. He'd given me his reasons on the front, the day before the battle, and she described to me the pain his actions had caused.

"She told me about her life, her mother who'd never married and had only one child in a land where families often had a dozen. After she'd been abandoned, pregnant, she'd withdrawn in shame, falling into a depression that lasted all her life. She'd named her daughter Riva, after *rive*, the word for coast, because it was the coast that had brought her father, whom she still loved.

"Riva Dubé also suffered abandonment. She married a man, and after three years without bearing him a child, he went to work in Nashua, a town where French was so common the immigrant workers had no need for English. She followed him there a year later and found that he'd remarried. Riva—your mother—lived as the second wife, cleaning rooms in a hotel. He became ill with a wasting sickness, and after his death, she returned to her village in Québec. My letter was waiting for her in the post office. But she also learned that her mother had had a second daughter, out of wedlock, and the girl—having grown up an outsider—ended up working in Montréal's brothels and cabarets. Riva tried to track her down and eventually learned that she'd been killed. Drunken, demented soldiers back from the war—a few of them from her own village—had raped and murdered her with broken bottles,

and then fought among themselves, cutting and blinding each
other. Hearing the villagers speak of those men as heroes, Riva
couldn't bear the idea of staying. The people in the village didn't
even believe her sister was dead, but that, in her sin and suffering,
she'd found God at last, since that was how all stories should end.
Riva left, traveling to the return address on the letter. She thought
she was barren. She was nearly forty but still looked like a girl.

"For her, I conjured from my memory the life her father had
told me. It took me weeks to bring it all back. Riva held the violin
she'd heard so much about. And then one night she left the place
where she'd been sleeping across the room, and she lay with me.
How can I explain this to you? We were both filled with the ten-
derness of people who have stopped measuring the world against
their hopes but who have come to see what is simply before them.
I was glad to have met her then, because I had healed enough to
touch her with a steady hand."

As Father and I returned to our familiar mountains, he spoke.
My world had changed, composed now of men wounded in distant
fields, on different continents. They carried each other's bodies
and then stories.

A few months after our walk together, I heard Father go out
to dance. He'd made a little more sound in the night, his footsteps
heavier, the door closing unevenly. He came in at the usual hour,
when silver light lined the mountains. He curled up next to Mama.
She held his head to her chest and stroked his hair. After a while,
she stood. She moved her fingers once beneath each eye. That was
all the grief I ever saw. She pulled the sheet over his head and told
me to go outside with her.

———

In the weeks that followed, I learned that Father had invested
every penny he'd earned in land. He'd bought up the mountain

slopes around him and eventually sold them to companies building ski resorts. He then bought more land and sold it to the people who wanted luxury homes in the mountains nearby. We lived in a one-room cabin until I was eighteen, and he was among the richest men in town. Mama explained it to me by saying that he'd had nothing else to do. He'd been earning money for forty years and didn't see much use in putting it in a bank.

Mama managed his accounts and gave me an allowance to study in New York.

It was 1963, and upon my arrival, I immediately became intoxicated with the wildness of that time. I listened to Bob Dylan and read *On the Road*. I kept taking my allowance but not the classes. I played the violin with whoever would join me, but it was an instrument of the bourgeoisie, I decided, not suited for the times—at least not one that could be at the center of it all. People wanted words and ideas, and with the notion that old things had to perish to make way for the new, I pawned the violin and walked out of the shop with a guitar. I wrote my first song, "Pawning the War." I didn't know it yet but in its lyrics I was already grieving what I'd lost.

I traveled the country. I stopped going by Joseph, introducing myself as Joe. I lived in communes and forest camps. I spent a month in a desert, its silence a deep, resonant hum: the sound of my own blood made apparent. I slept on floors and rooftops in cities, and played in bars for money, as if I were broke. My friends were being drafted for Vietnam, and I was eventually called up. I wrote "Canada Waiting," "Going North," "Crossing the Line."

I loved Canada. I believed the story of its goodness: uncontaminated, the end of the Underground Railroad. I mostly loved the nude beaches and plentiful drugs, the company of expats whose favorite topic was the failure we'd abandoned to the south. Then the war ended, and people showed up less and less, stopped cheering or chanting to songs. Music was suddenly just music—something for the background.

I told myself that I was finally composing my best lyrics now that I had no audience. I wrote "In His Blood" and "Dead Man on the Tracks" and "A Song from Faraway." I was trying to recreate what I'd been resisting and all that I'd left.

*That's when you knew—*
*Your story was a bullet coming for you.*

Mother died, and I couldn't go back for the funeral. I hired a lawyer to handle the details, to figure out how to transfer my wealth to me. After "A Song from Faraway," I stopped writing lyrics. Even that song, I played only once.

*You knew it the first time you read about war,*
*the first time you fucked a girl in your father's car,*
*the first time your mama said you were a boy,*
*the first time you fought your brother for a toy.*
*You felt the bullet in your mother's womb.*
*You lay in your crib like a hero in a tomb.*
*That's how it is to remember,*
*to be born with a sense of who you were.*

I realized I'd been strumming the same chords for a decade. I'd been talking loudly to the rhythm of a borrowed sound. So I put the guitar away for good and used the lyrics of my last song for the opening to a novel by the same name.

My first novel ended up being my last, not because I didn't write another one. During the years that I couldn't finish it, I wrote others and published them. The reviews were good, the sales barely respectable—sufficient for my ego, though not for a living. I had my inheritance for that.

In my books, I recreated the country I'd abandoned through the stories passed down to me—wars, burnings, lynchings, my

grandfather's bone fob, Wounded Knee. At readings, friends listened, distracted. Reviewers suggested I dial it back. I recalled my
father's memory of Estrada's story, and I wrote it with care, certain
that this might be the beginning of something new, but afterward,
when I read it, I wasn't sure what it was. I kept waiting for the
rest of it to come, to turn into a novel, but it didn't. One day I
understood. I had written only the piece that had been transmitted
to me, but I'd never been south of Tijuana. I was an old white man
in a basement den in Vancouver, smoking myself into emphysema.

I tucked the story away in my books. When I stepped back,
there was no sign that it was there. I wondered if someone would
find it and who it would be—maybe a grad student perusing
whichever archives these scribblings ended up in. Definitely not
my wife or son. I liked the idea of leaving this little mystery, another piece of our family for someone who cared enough to put it
back together.

One afternoon, returning from the bar, I dropped in on a fellow writer. He'd recently married one of his students, and only she
was home. As we waited for my friend to get back, she and I talked
for hours in the kitchen. I told her about the story, about waiting
for the inspiration to make it into something bigger—my masterpiece maybe. I knew this would never happen, but I liked how it
sounded and felt good talking about it. She finally told me that my
friend was out of town, giving a reading in Toronto. She and I had
sex on the couch, the table, the bed. She got pregnant and moved
in with me, but she soon figured out that I didn't believe in my
own words. We never again captured the rawness of our encounter, the power of that chance crossing. She had a boy. I lived in the
basement, trying to untangle history. Being a man seemed to mean
that you wandered, you searched, you escaped, you woke up half-
dead in a field or by train tracks. But I had nowhere to go, nothing
to die for on the way to reaching it. I nurtured the idea of myself as
the final resister. I chain-smoked and read in my basement study.

*A Song from Faraway,* I told myself, would be my keystone work, but I didn't finish it until after Samantha. I picked her up on the highway. She'd driven from Virginia to Alaska to find the father she'd never known, a pipeline worker who, when she met him, kept hitting on her, seemingly incapable of comprehending that she was his daughter. On her way back, her car died. We spent a week in a motel, drinking beer and smoking dope, eating and making love. My entire life curved around the gravity of those days. She'd grown up nearly two thousand miles from where I had, but she felt like home.

And then, when I came back from a beer run, she was gone. I never saw her again. I don't know why I couldn't forget her. She'd been in my life too briefly for me to call what I was feeling grief, but that's what it was.

I finally finished my first novel, about a composer of protest songs who has lost his audience—"My best work," I told everyone, but the reviewers had already grown bored of me. I was reiterating, they said, objecting to wars that were best forgotten.

I stayed in my basement study. The key to the future I was searching for always felt close. I thought of the melody my grandfather whistled, that my father recognized when my other grandfather played it on the front. I thought of it and cried. I had never heard it though I felt I had.

# Killing the Man

On a Sunday afternoon, armed riders arrived at the
orphanage and lined the older boys up outside the
wall. A stout man with an oiled mustache selected the
fittest of them, picking León last. The nuns prayed as the boys
were led away, along a dusty path.

The revolution had begun three years before, and hanging
about in the street, León had heard men discuss battles throughout the country whose size and shape and location he could not
fathom. Porfirio Díaz had lost power and gone into exile, and
Francisco Madero had assumed the presidency but his general,
Victoriano Huerta, had him killed. Despite such talk, León's sense
of war remained childish—a dim figure in bloody garments shot
down in the red dust a thousand times.

Now it seemed he was to play a part in it. The stout man explained that their job was to run cans of dynamite to the windows
of barracks or to any group of Federales.

"Don't throw until you are at the window," he told them, "or
until you see this. The white stuff." He lowered his face and pointed
at the bloodshot jelly of his eye.

On their first attack, running barefoot over hot earth as
Federales fired and were fired upon by Zapata's men, bullets hissing past from all directions, boys perished. Shot, they collapsed

and went up in flame and smoke, or they threw too late and had their faces blasted off. But León persisted, weaving like a jackrabbit, running in can after can.

Though he outlasted the other boys, he resented the men who'd turned him into living artillery. They went about in boots and with hats to shade their faces, and after battles, they looted, gathering weapons and food. Though thirteen, León appeared younger, with a curved spine and the ribs of a sick dog. His eyes felt larger than his head: studying the world, looking up—examining faces, discerning the workings of power and respect.

The dynamite boys became a regular crew. Zapata had stripped mining camps of their dynamite to overcome his lack of artillery. Other commanders employed a similar technique, the *máquina loca*, a train engine loaded with explosives and sent chugging into towns. But the *dinamiteros* were more versatile. When the enemy were dug in or gathered behind wagons and walls, the boys were greased and sent out like dark elves holding lethal sparklers. Or to initiate surprise attacks, they wandered into town with piñatas and toys stuffed with dynamite and tossed them through barrack windows while Zapata's men remained hidden, waiting to see roof tiles rise into the sky like a deck of cards.

But in battle, the Federales kept watch, taking aim. As León sprinted and dodged, bullets ticked past, measuring every second.

Then a horse bowled him over. The can fell and rolled beyond his grasp, into a stand of cacti, its fuse burning wildly.

The world went dark as if someone had slammed a door on the sky.

———

León came to in a field of dead men. His skin was raw. Blood crusted his eyes and ears. Everything was silent: the wind against his wounds, the crows swaggering above the dead, his battering, grateful heart.

Crouched next to him was a very old man with black eyebrows and a grizzled beard. From León's years as an orphan, he could read faces, had known, with a glance, which vendors would curse at him and which ones might give him a slice of papaya. He'd seen indifference in the soldiers who'd made him run dynamite, and kindness now in the face of the man above him, who eased León up and led him from the field.

Not until weeks later, when León could hear again, did he learn that the old man was from faraway. His name was Kyros, and he spoke in an accent that made him sound as if he were laughing at his own words. He nursed León to health in an abandoned monastery whose prickly pears he cultivated and whose walls he'd freshly decorated with an array of Madonnas. He told stories of traveling the world, painting icons for pay, on ships' masts and sails, on saddles and gunstocks and hearths, once even on each of the breasts of a teenaged widow who hoped to cross through the Zangezur Mountains back to her childhood village in Armenia without being raped, or if raped, then not killed.

Arriving in Mexico, he had been transfixed by the image of the Virgin of Guadalupe. He began painting her as he had before, on weapons and clothes and homes. His more eclectic customers he invited to the monastery to show them the Madonnas on the walls, what one man called a harem of Virgins, a comment Kyros received grimly. But as if at a brothel in a port city, clients chose from Greek, Russian, Italian, and local varieties. When these men praised him as a great artist, Kyros showed his few teeth but didn't nod. Alone with León, he explained his reticence.

"Artists," he said in the tone used for thieves or liars, "they sign their names on their work as if they have made it or own it. But what does God not make?"

When León was well, Kyros taught him to read properly, finishing the work that the nuns had begun. He had only two books in Spanish, the dictionary and the Bible, both with disintegrated bindings.

"Do not mix their pages," he warned. "We must not confuse the two sorts of truth. If we begin looking to the dictionary for inspiration and the Bible for reality, we will surely go mad."

The sun-bleached walls of the ruined monastery were just beyond the capital, and the men who hired Kyros discussed how the Americans had blockaded Mexico in order to cut off supplies for the Germans, and how the economy was suffering. They spoke of General Pershing who'd invaded Chihuahua to pursue Pancho Villa. They hoped for safety against the factionalism and lawlessness here and therefore commissioned murals of the Virgin for protection. Because her symbol had been taken up by so many of the contesting forces who had stolen their banners from the altars of churches, the churches themselves commissioned reproductions.

Though León's hand was not as steady with the brush as it was with dynamite, he learned to sketch outlines that Kyros filled in and brought to life, all the while mumbling the rules of painting— most importantly that one must never inscribe his personality on a holy image.

His Virgins exuded compassion the depth of which León had not seen even in the orphanage nuns. Customers stared at Kyros's walls in awe and reverence. In this way, with León's help, Kyros earned more and they lived well, buying blankets and staples and the eucalyptus that Kyros rubbed on his joints and inhaled to clear his lungs.

———

Early one morning, a young woman arrived at the monastery. One hand held a long, dusty pistol, the other pressed below her breast, as if she were steadying herself to shoot. She made Kyros and León feed her at gunpoint but refused to let the old man treat her wound. She lay down and asked for water and, with the gun trained on them, fell asleep.

"Do not take the gun away," Kyros said. "She must know that we are not enemies."

When she came to with a start, Kyros pointed out that she'd slept. She wanted to know whose side they were on. Kyros said, "God," and León said he did not believe in sides.

"Perhaps someday God," the old man said.

"Perhaps," León replied.

"Painting the image of the Holy Mother might convert you. That is the purpose."

"Perhaps," he mumbled.

This exchange and their lack of sides bothered the woman, and she later explained that she'd followed her husband into battle to cook and care for him, and after he was shot down, she took his gun and became a *soldadera*. Her group had been decimated and she'd tried to return home, but she and the few survivors had been attacked in the night. Her face, gaunt and creased and bronzed from the sun, suggested Indigenous blood and a woman much older than her seventeen years. She'd married three years before and had lost two children in childbirth and now her husband. Her name was Anna.

Though she kept the gun with her at all times, she agreed to let Kyros treat her wound. A bullet had passed through the flesh of her side, breaking a rib without striking her lung.

Once mended, Anna was a better painter than León, but over the next two years, when Kyros encouraged her to read, she said, "I cannot waste my time on words when there is a war to be fought."

Though she didn't leave, on occasion she spoke of land redistribution, ideas she was clearly repeating, for she said them in the same way each time. She accepted Kyros's lack of political alignment because he was Greek, but León's absence of passion angered her. When she caught him looking at her, she sneered.

"You ugly mongrel, there is nothing I like about you. If you get any ideas about my hole, I will shoot a hole in you so that you can enjoy yourself."

The creases had begun to fade from her face, and with nourishment her expression had become less gaunt. She looked more and more like a girl.

Late that April, she and León were preparing a mural on an iron merchant's house. Kyros remained at the monastery to rest his arthritic joints and would join them each afternoon to add the finishing touches. With just an hour, he could make their day of work into something beautiful. But he didn't arrive. They returned to the monastery and found him on the bed, the shine gone from his dark eyes, a bullet hole in his chest.

Without words or tears, they buried him beneath white stone from a fallen wall.

They fasted that night, in the cold, their food and money and blankets all stolen.

The next day they attempted to finish the mural, but the man who had hired Kyros would not pay for their shoddy work and the lack of love in the Virgin's eyes. No matter how many lines he and Anna painted over and redrew, they could not create the impression of forgiveness that the old man had so easily achieved.

———

Once, while Kyros had been painting, he had said, "You two children must take care of each other. You are all that you have in this world."

Anna had not responded, and León had been confused as to whom Kyros was speaking, as there were no children nearby.

Then he understood. He was tempted to announce how many men he'd killed. For as long as he recalled, he'd had to fight for respect—as a dynamite boy and, before that, an orphan. When the nuns had told him that he'd been left on the granite step on March 2nd, 1900—the pope's first birthday in the new century—and had been named in his honor, he'd been proud, as if he might also be respected. Since living with Kyros, he'd grown out of his stunted figure, not tall but learning to carry himself like a man.

His gaze, though, was still that of a child, his dark eyes too open, too clear in their assessment of the world. Sleepless, he remained unsure of carnal relations. His only knowledge of the union between men and women was that soldiers rode into villages, dismounted, and dragged shrieking girls from houses, tossed them on the ground and got on top of them, kicking their legs apart while pushing down their own pants. It looked like an easy enough thing to do and the men left with great satisfaction and laughter, usually taking with them a few hens or a goat, but the girls did not seem to enjoy it so much, and as the men were leaving, some of the girls remained in the dust, arms and legs splayed, as if they had fallen from a great height.

He knew that if he were to try such a thing with Anna, she would shoot him. And with Kyros dead, she declared that she would return to the war. But she did nothing. The next morning she said she would go back to her village, but she remained.

The capital was an hour's walk and each day he looked for work. The streets bustled with merchants and mercenaries: European faces scowling down from horses and Indigenous ones clustered on street corners, squinting up with distrust. While loitering at the dog fights, he learned that the civil war and general lawlessness had created a thriving market in assassinations and vendettas, and he wished he could ask Anna for her gun.

When there were arguments, he approached the angry party and suggested that the other man should suffer.

"Anger is not violence," one dog trainer told him. "Go away, you idiot, before I shoot you."

But others were less philosophical. León stabbed a fat tortilla merchant and strangled a thug with a wire.

A week of hunger made killing easier than he'd expected. The ugliness of the world seemed its only certainty, not the hope or trust that Kyros had awakened in him.

If only he'd painted as well as he murdered.

———

After the war died down but for the occasional skirmish, brigandage and influenza continued to inflict suffering. In 1919, President Carranza had Zapata assassinated at Chinameca, the news bringing grief to peasants and celebrations in the capital. Shortly afterward, Carranza's general, Obregón, declared his presidential candidacy. Carranza planned to have him killed, but Obregón rebelled, and this time it was Carranza who fled. In May of 1920, the great implacable Carranza was shot dead in a hut in Puebla.

Though the ten-year war appeared to be over, León continued to kill. He could now identify, just from reading men's expressions, those who were angry enough to have someone murdered. But the competition was fierce, the pay poor, and assassinations were even contracted on the barter system.

One afternoon, having settled a land dispute with a knife, he returned with a pale chunk of fatty-looking material he'd received in a sack with rice and beans and tortillas.

"Is this food?" he asked Anna.

She laughed. "It's soap, you idiot."

His orphanage had been too poor for such a luxury, and she herself had seen it only on rare occasions. She held it to her nose as she walked down to the stream.

The sun was setting when she returned, rusty pine needles clinging to her feet. There, as she climbed the path between trees, beyond the rough shapes of the ruins, he saw her as a fresco, sketched out against the shadows, the skin of her face bright, her cheekbones wide and her full lashes transforming her eyes into dark suns. Desperately, he wanted to touch her skin—to do something, anything—run to the wall of Madonnas and strip away their cloaks and press his lips to their breasts.

Though he said nothing—revealed nothing—this longing brought with it the urge to make more money and be more successful. In the days that followed, at the races and in bars, he inquired constantly about work, studying faces.

"I know of a serious job," a one-eyed man told him, "with serious people who pay serious money. But in order to apply, you have to know how to read."

———

The officer wore a brown suit and a collarless shirt and stood at a table on which sat seven identical books. A Remington pistol hung from his thick leather belt, and his mustache hunched on his lip, his teeth as gapped and irregular as a crude horse comb. His eyes were as black and deep as gun barrels, moving in imperceptible increments.

"You *pendejos* are gathered here today," he said in a phlegmy voice, "to kill a man. An elusive and intelligent son of a whore. You look like idiots to me, so I suspect that none of you will succeed. And if you have lied and you cannot read, I will send you out this door with the farewell of my boot on your ignorant ass."

As he explained the contract, the seven hit men stood, a few in military stance, one in a black cowboy suit, the rest ragged and skinny, León himself the leanest.

The man said that their target, a certain Rafael María Estrada, had authored the book whose copies sat on the table.

"This book is said to be his life's work and mentions all of the places he has lived. I will give each of you a copy. If you can find the *hijo de puta* without it, then may the Virgin bless you. If not, you must study it to learn where he is hiding. I will give you a small sum for these efforts, but the man who finds him will be well rewarded."

Under the scrutiny of the officer in the brown suit, each of the hit men went up, took a copy and read a few lines out loud, like schoolchildren.

Afterward, they received a pouch of coins as well as a sketch of Estrada's handsome mug and information concerning his land holdings: a sheet of addresses and a map on which each was marked with an *X*.

"We will be checking in on you," the officer said. "We have made a note of where to find you, and if we think that you're not making an effort, we will visit you. Killing is cheap these days. Cheaper than what I'm paying you now."

León took the fat tome, as substantial as a Bible, though less weathered. The dirty, threadbare cotton of his shirt clung to his damp ribs. He was suddenly sweating with hunger. In the dim room, a constellation of determined eyes hovered about him, and he wanted his own stars to shine with such certain and indifferent light.

————

*The Angels Write Poetry with Blood* was the title of the tome, whose pages numbered 783. This was the first book that wasn't the Bible, the dictionary, or a guide to catechism that León had read. He explained the job to Anna who snorted and said, "That is so stupid. Who reads books to kill men?"

The work was slow going, and it took him a day to finish the first three pages, though on the second he read nine and on the third, twenty. He moved his lips over each sentence, then read it aloud once before testing it in his mind. He paused often to check the dictionary, perplexed as to who used words such as *adamantine* or *loquacious*.

*His adamantine refusal to let me speak,* the author wrote. *My loquacious father.*

The father in question was Mexican born but denied any *Indio* blood, claiming that his dusky skin resulted from Andalusian taint. What adulteration his lineage had suffered he remedied by marrying the author's German mother. Blond and blue-eyed, she knew little Spanish and was forbidden to use her own language, so never spoke. The father was in politics and wanted his son to boast perfect Spanish. He was afraid to encumber the boy's tongue with guttural tones and had chosen her simply for her unusual pallor, as if she were water with which to rinse his scalded arteries.

"What a monster!" Anna announced.

León had not realized she was listening as he stumbled through each sentence. She joined him on the cot, adjusting her gun belt so that the pistol was not in the way.

"All of that is in this book?" she asked.

"Yes, and much more it would seem."

He was only on page fifty-three.

"Keep telling the story," she said.

With this request, his confidence grew. He read, pausing less frequently to check the dictionary and noting references to the Bible that he recalled from his lessons with Kyros. The words that Anna might not know he simply changed.

"My father," he read, "taught me to use anyone for my goals. He slept with beautiful women, brought them home under my mother's nose, often dark women, and sent them away with a few coins. If they returned with babies, he denied parentage. From him, I learned that all causes are but to further one's primacy, to make men fear you and women long for you. But as I came of age, he and I had our own struggle for primacy. I did not agree with his politics and wrote pamphlets under pseudonyms in support of his political enemies, though I later denied those books and those names and denied the women I'd enjoyed when I wrote and lived under those names. Largely by accident, I found my calling as a journalist for American papers, and my contacts in the United

States obliged me to maintain an identity for longer than a few months. On my first visit, they treated me as a hero who didn't fear to speak out against tyranny. That was amusing. I loved the women there, so casual in how they threw away their honor."

León paused as Anna shook her head. "He is as horrible as his father, and yet such a man. So brave. So willing to do what pleases him." She touched León's arm and looked into his eyes. "He will change, won't he?"

"Wait. Listen," León told her. "Though I befriended whoever could help me further my reputation, I began to nurture the idea of myself as a man who strove to make the world a better place. I was not for the communists because Americans did not approve of such things. I simply wanted what they did: true democracy and all that was supposed to come with it. I felt that I sought a worthy cause, and briefly, writing my tracts, I believed that I was the voice of struggle, that by my words alone I would liberate Mexico of the tyrants who, like my father, had oppressed it. You could say that I became the man whom I lied about being. I invented a history and liked it enough to forget the old one. I seduced myself with the character I had created: heroic and driven, passionate yet flawed by his lust for life. I dreamed of being an admired author. I chose only the fights I could win. I mistreated only those women who would not tell and loved tenderly only those who would speak of it. I had a corrupt character, and since character is destiny, true of men as it is of their nations, I expected disaster.

"My trouble came of a pet notion I had. I fancied that by consorting with many women I was creating a superior breed. I sought adulterous unions with the wives of powerful men, imagining that the leaders of our country would be raising my sons. But to be caught in bed, my arms around a woman's narrow waist, my lips on her breast—to be seen and apprehended in that way—transformed me instantly from a despoiler to a suckling babe soon to be torn from its blind pleasure.

"The general, her husband, had his men tie me up. He gashed my forehead with the butt of his pistol. He punched my face until his wedding band split and fell off, and then he appeared somewhat satisfied. His wife had been taken away by guards, and I could hear her shrieking down the hall. Eventually, she fell silent, around the moment the wedding band broke. It was then that I realized I had but one skill. Through the veil of blood on my face, I negotiated for my life.

'Just as you are transforming me, I can transform you,' I said.

'You are threatening me?' the general asked.

'No. I can write you. I can make the Americans call you a hero. Your enemies will fear you, and the peasants who rally against you will praise you. What does it matter if I die today or tomorrow or next year?'

"The general gave this some thought. We discussed the details, that he would keep me imprisoned and that if my writing defamed him, he would torture and kill me.

"During the months I spent in that cell, I learned a great deal about myself. I was not brave. I had taken no decisive actions and lived hidden by words. Yes, my writings were saving me, but each page of propaganda was the soiled bill with which I purchased another day. The general mocked me. He denigrated the work I had formerly done. And yet, in composing his life, I came to understand him. This is the purpose of art, I saw. We blend with others. We glimpse what else we might become. I saw traces of myself in his laudatory biography, and I knew that he, in reading it, perceived himself differently. I wrote him as a hero, and he became more heroic. Gradually, he took up new causes and abandoned old ones. He saw me as a compatriot and freed me from my cell. Not long afterward his old allies turned on him and had him killed. Even as I fled, I believed that the general had died a better man, and I at last saw the magic of my vocation. This terrified and elated me, and I decided to fight for those who were oppressed and to do so by making men see something better within themselves."

Anna was excited. "That is my cause he is fighting for. I am certain of it."

Though León should have been seeking Rafael María Estrada, he preferred telling this story. Each day, Anna sat closer or got up to paint the book's characters on the walls, naïvely evoking the author's father and the general on the chalky stone, their faces virginal and beatific.

But sitting in the monastery's white dust, in the sunlight near the prickly pears, León didn't know if a man could so completely change. Anna hung close and no longer called him a scrawny mutt, and with each of her smiles, the brutal indifferent world he'd known crumbled a little, as if it, too, had been painted on a ruined wall.

———

In the breeze, beyond the monastery gate, dust turned clockwise, like a dial. A rider was approaching. A harness jangled, hoofbeats reverberating between limestone. It was the officer in the brown suit.

"Have you made any progress?" he asked León. Anna stood just inside, her hand on the pistol, but though he glanced at her face, he ignored her.

"Yes," León said. "I have read much of the book and have been considering the places where he might be hiding."

"We have people throughout Mexico," the officer said. "One would think that he has escaped to the United States, but his news dispatches reveal that he is here. It should be easy to find him. He is blond and blue eyed. There are not so many of those. Unfortunately, one of our men shot a foreign envoy and was hanged. So be careful."

At that the officer rode back down the path.

In the days that followed, León read as Anna listened and painted. He described Estrada's encounter with his true love, a poetic woman whom he convinced not only of his goodness but of his cause. Since her parents' suspicious deaths when she was thirteen, she had been the ward of her uncle, a rich *norteño hacendado* despised by the revolutionaries. Far worse, the uncle had promised her hand in marriage to one of his allies in return for military protection. Though the revolutionaries had put a price on the uncle's head, Estrada fought him in a duel not for money but to free the woman he loved. They shot each other—the uncle killed, Estrada wounded in the chest. He lay in the field and forsook hope, accepting death. But a day later an itinerant madman stumbled upon him and helped him return home. The woman he loved nursed him back to health.

"Being wounded," he wrote, "I learned the helplessness of love, the way that our weaknesses open us to the world and deliver us to safety."

He married this woman, later claiming the bounty on her uncle as her dowry. Nights, as they lay together, she traced the circle of scar on his chest as if it were the ring with which he'd pledged his love.

"It is like me," Anna said with a dry voice, "when I came here and you took care of me."

She stared into León's face as though he had been the one to tend her wound.

She swallowed and wet her lips. "And? What happens next?"

"We must go," he told her. "We are running out of money. We must find him."

"But where is he?"

León turned away, afraid to read another of the five hundred remaining pages, afraid that Estrada would be corrupted again and ruin this love. He closed his eyes, thinking back through all that he had read.

"I know," he told her. "Yes, I see it. I am certain. But it is far."

With his love in his arms, Estrada had convinced her to accompany him to a secluded valley—not near the capital but near the

American border. The place wasn't marked on the map because Estrada didn't own the land. During a period of uncertainty after the general's death, he'd sought refuge from men. In his wanderings, he'd come upon the small valley in the mountains southwest of Nuevo Laredo, *a place close to the earth,* he wrote, *and yet so high above it—Indian trails through forest and ravine, paths that reveal more of the sky than the land. Because it is unnamed, it does not seem connected to the history and struggles of our country. It is closer to the sky's timeless blue.*

"You are so intelligent," Anna told him as they began packing their few things, the Bible and dictionary and the book. Anna went to the stream to bathe and then returned in her damp dress. She took him by the wrist.

"You must also bathe," she said.

He followed her, drunk with her touch.

The bar of soap sat on a rock, and he stepped into the cold current and faced away, stripping his clothes. He flinched as the soap brushed his back. Her fingers rested on his shoulder and turned him toward her and moved down along his chest.

Holding his wrist, she led him back to the monastery. She unbuckled her gun belt and gave it to him. Then she pulled off her dress and lay on the cot and reached for his hand.

———

To earn extra money for the journey, León hired himself out to a loan shark and strangled a debtor in an alley. He took the man's horse and, with Anna behind him, rode north. Though in the past the ugliness of men had blinded him to the task of killing, he felt disturbed. That night and into the next day, as they rode steadily, he thought of the debtor, wondering if within him there had been the possibility of change.

"Someone is following us," Anna told him late that afternoon.

Figures wavered in and out of sight against the horizon, far back on the road, never gaining. On arid flats, after the sun had fallen past the horizon, the refracted light lifted the figures into mirage-like projections: seven lean riders set against the dimming sky, their horses elongated so as to appear on stilts.

Though León and Anna slept a ways from the road, their followers never passed. The journey took nearly two weeks, the horse struggling over cracked, sun-bombed plains, the roadway scattered with broken bits of rock as if strewn with bullets and sometimes with actual bullet casings. Sweating, they pulled blankets against their backs and over their heads to fend off the sun. Midday, their shadow plumbed the earth, dark as a well, making León think of fresh water. And yet he would have been content had the ride lasted forever, Anna's arms around his waist, his body swaying in the saddle like a man's.

They left the road well before Nuevo Laredo and traveled through pine forests. That night, after they had made love on their blankets, León lay and listened to wolves howling in the mountains, to the fluting of night birds and bat wings skittering above treetops.

Kyros had once said, "Reading is a conversation with other men, wiser than those we often meet on this bloodied earth. That is the beauty of a written word. Even a prisoner condemned to death can communicate beyond his loneliness to the one person who longs to hear him countries and centuries away."

He'd spoken of books as living things and once, in Egypt, had seen a Jewish funeral and asked who had died only to learn that they were burying a damaged Torah. "But they weren't crying," he'd added. "Probably because they had other copies."

Lying with Anna beneath the twilight, León wished he could continue the book. He feared meeting Estrada, whose story he'd put on like a suit.

They came upon the valley their first morning in the mountains.

"This is the place," he said upon cresting the rise. The book described a pale jut of stone like a castle's turret, and León had studied the words *castle* and *turret* in the disheveled pages of the dictionary until he could picture such things. The landmark was easily visible from the foot of the mountains, exposed like a white flag.

The climb from the hilly lands below was steeper than it had first appeared. The pine forest pressed in upon the trail, freeing them from the sun, and the sky was a flashing, jagged path between treetops. Insects clouded, darting at their faces, and despite the shade León perspired. His hands trembled.

At the next rise, the small valley opened. A fast-moving stream spread out along its floor, shallow and rippling over its many rocks, the water glittering like sequined cloth. Beneath the pale turret stood a log cabin.

When they reached the stream, León dismounted and stumbled into the current, light-headed, soaked with sweat. He splashed his face.

"*No puedo,*" he said. "I cannot kill him."

He removed the gun belt and put it on a stone and pulled off his shirt and plunged into the brisk water, gasping.

"Killing should be simple," he sobbed, but when he looked up, Anna was staring past him, to the edge of the forest. Her features were gaunt, the broad lines of her jaw and cheekbones prominent. Her eyes moved to the gun on the stone.

"Reach for the gun and I will shoot," a man said from the forest. He was crouched behind a large pine, holding a rifle. His face was that of the sketch León had carried for weeks.

Tall, his square head topped with hair the color of sun-blanched sand, Estrada stood and stared. His gray eyes suggested a colder sky, windy and sunless, about to rain. He kept his rifle trained on them.

"You do not seem like killers," he said. "I heard what you said about not being able to kill me. Why? Why are you not able?"

"Because of your book," León told him.

"Yes," Anna said, "the story is so beautiful."

"You've read my book?" Estrada raised his pale eyebrows. He cradled his rifle absentmindedly. "Is the country lawless enough that even critics set out after authors?"

He laughed, showing his white teeth and exposing the untanned line of his throat, pale like that of a deer.

Anna and León glanced at each other with incomprehension.

"You really read my book?" Estrada asked again. "Really? That's wonderful. So why then have you come?"

León took a deep breath. "To warn you," he said and explained why he had been hired and that other men were following them on the long road from the capital.

"Men following?" Estrada repeated, suddenly ashen. He splashed into the stream and took León's gun belt and slung it over his shoulder. "I will get my manuscript. Then we must ride for Laredo. We have to reach the border before it's too late."

---

The journey to Nuevo Laredo was swift along the path that Estrada took them. León had gathered courage to ask about the book, and Estrada answered while glancing behind. He kept his horse close to theirs, perhaps for cover.

He rarely stopped talking. No wonder he had written so many pages, but at least those had been well considered. He spoke about Anna and León, their oddness: hardened children, killers who read the books of their victims. As they cantered north, it seemed that if he hadn't shot them, it was because he liked talking so much.

León interrupted him. "What are we going to do?"

Estrada reached into a saddlebag and took out a crushed panama hat, knocked some shape into it, and then set it on his head at a rakish angle. He told them that they should escape to America and that he would give them some money.

The thought of fleeing Mexico had been beyond the reach of León's mind, but now he grasped the power of change described in Estrada's book. Reading it, he had seen the shape of Mexico for the first time and understood the nature of the conflict that had not yet resolved at the time of writing. Until then, war's movement over the landscape had been invisible to him, approaching as clouds might, appearing suddenly on the horizon. Through the book, he'd seen the borders of nations and oceans as if observing the planet from the vantage of the moon.

When Nuevo Laredo came into sight, Estrada unloaded his rifle and threw it into the ditch. They rode through the busy streets to the crossing, where he told the American guards that he was a journalist for a New York paper and that León and Anna were his assistants. Once across, he appeared to relax. He had their horses kept at a stable, and at the train station, he purchased three tickets and bought sweet sodas for León and Anna.

"Fresher than water," she told Léon, and he finished the sentence—"but like honey." They consumed their drinks in quick sips.

Estrada kept glancing along the crowded platform. The train arrived and they took their seats as, just below, a soda vendor passed. Anna asked if she could buy another. Léon wanted one as well. Estrada tossed her a coin and told her to get three of them, but to hurry.

"She is your wife?" he asked Léon.

"I don't know."

"Really? That's interesting. Are you waiting for a priest to tell you?"

When Léon didn't answer, Estrada narrowed his eyes.

"How amazing. You really don't know, do you?"

León had never considered this, so much of his mind empty, as if his thoughts journeyed, as had he and Anna, through deserts.

"In any case, I appreciate your help," Estrada said. "With the war over, I didn't expect those military men to seek vengeance. They won, after all."

The whistle sounded and the train gave a jerk and started to move.

"Where is she anyway?" Estrada asked as they turned toward the window.

On the platform, the black-clad cowboy, one of the hit men from that first meeting with the officer, stood with a group of men, two of whom were pulling Anna's arms behind her back and cuffing them. She struggled against them and shouted León's name as the train pulled from the station, gaining speed.

If León had not run to save Anna, it was because he knew that only by bringing Estrada back would she be released. And Estrada himself confirmed this.

"They want me," he said. "Wait. Let me think this through. I'll find a solution."

León had no doubt that he would. Estrada was the author of *The Angels Write Poetry with Blood*. He had survived and prevailed in worse circumstances. But as the train labored farther from Mexico, León lost certainty, not just in Estrada, but in why he himself had not run to help Anna.

"What will we do?" he asked after a few minutes. Estrada was sitting, his chin on his fist and his hand on the butt of his pistol. He looked up.

"Have you been on a train before?"

"No."

"But you must know how they work, right?"

"No, I do not."

"It's quite simple. Trains travel in large circles. This one will go east, then north, then west and south again. It is a journey of one day. Then we will arrive back in Laredo. The men who have Anna know this and will be waiting. All we can do then is fight."

León considered the mystery and convenience of circular train routes, wondering if it might make more sense for them to run in straight lines, like roads.

"So you will give me my gun then?" he asked.

"Of course," Estrada said and took the belt from where he'd stashed it inside a saddlebag. He handed the pistol back, along with a jacket.

"Put this on and keep the gun hidden. The jacket will make you look American."

León did as he was told, amazed at the courage and intelligence of this author. Estrada also offered him a white silk scarf, and later, to expend his restless energy, León walked through the train, feeling substantial and taller, no different from the well-dressed passengers who glanced up as he paced.

---

All day, the train shook north, and the calm that the new garments had endowed began to fade. As panic set in, León held his head, thinking of Anna and what the men would do to her if he didn't return soon. Estrada appeared calm, staring out the window, the sunset cooling in the gray of his eyes.

Gradually, as night occupied the plains of Texas, a terrible thought took shape. León hadn't finished the book. He couldn't be certain that Estrada had truly changed and no longer used people.

At San Antonio and Austin, the train stopped at stations lit with electric bulbs, and much later, as dawn dimmed the stars, they reached Fort Worth. Estrada had taken a manuscript from his bag, tied it with a string and put it inside his jacket, holding it against his side. He'd pulled his hat low and fallen asleep.

Along the platform, a man led a well-dressed woman who walked just behind him like a prize racehorse. Such a woman would never want León, not as Anna had. León lifted the impossibly soft material of the scarf and brushed it against his cheek.

Light appeared in the east. Exhaustion made his mind clear. He considered trains and that if they traveled in circles, then the circles must be truly immense. Estrada had no doubt lied and yet he slept there, easily, as if they were friends. He'd given him the gun and a fine serge jacket and this strange scarf.

Desperation, León's angel, brought him a thought. A man could lie convincingly about simple things, such as the nature of trains, but to lie about his book would be difficult, and one lie would bring the others tumbling down.

"I must confess something," he told Estrada, waking him. "I have read only two hundred and fifty-four pages of your book. In them, you changed, but what happens next? Did you find a better path and stay in love with the woman for whom you fought the duel?"

Estrada wiped a bit of drool from his cheek.

"Of course," he said. "The last five hundred pages detail my pursuit of a better life and the many challenges I faced and overcame, and my happy marriage."

Though León had only recently learned to read books, he'd spent a lifetime reading men's faces.

"You are lying," he said.

Estrada sighed and shook his head.

"Men," he said, "do not always become perfect when they try."

"But you are not good at all, are you?" León told him, suddenly enraged.

"Listen." Estrada shifted his posture to one of readiness. "Does the girl matter?"

"What do you mean?"

"Do you love her?"

"I don't know."

"Then it's not love," Estrada said with a satisfied look. "I can tell you this. If you do not feel love for her now, then you never will. It's futile. I've definitely tried, and if the love is not there in the beginning, it never is. You are in America now. Life is breathtaking here. I will help you start over. The possibilities are endless. Besides, would she risk her life for you? You know—don't tell me you don't—that if she found a wealthy man or a better opportunity, she would leave you."

The sun reached the green plains as the train bore down on Tulsa, its proximity announced on a large sign. Estrada alternately watched León's face and eyed the window.

"And I can get you any woman you want," Estrada told him. "You see the white women on this train. I will pay them to spread their legs for you. They have blond hairs down there, you know, as on their heads."

Oddly, black smoke was billowing into the sky above Tulsa. The train didn't stop, and passengers stared out at a conflagration just beyond the downtown. The whistle blew and the engine chugged toward the open lands.

"Life in America is good," he continued, looking suddenly worried. "You will have a whole house full of clothes better than my own."

León was considering all that Estrada had shared of himself in the book, how it had infused León, bonded them, just as Kyros had said that two men who read the Bible will speak with greater harmony. But perhaps one man's writing could corrupt another. León tried to imagine his future and suddenly, startlingly, he felt Anna's touch. Estrada stiffened in his seat as León sat up, vividly recalling Anna bathing his chest.

Their guns were out at the same moment. León raged at his own corruptibility.

Estrada was pale. "You are a paid killer," he said, "so I will not assume that I can outshoot you. Just tell me what you want."

The rest of the passengers had stood and gone to the windows on the other side of the train, distracted by Tulsa's burning buildings.

León realized that Estrada's astounding fear came of his belief that he was face to face with a skilled hit man. Hoping to take advantage of this, León attempted to sound tough. "How far is it back to Laredo?" he grunted.

"A day on horseback, maybe more," Estrada said. "But listen, I will go and talk to the train operator and tell him to turn the train around."

"He can do that?" León asked, trying to conceal his hope.

"Of course. For emergencies. There are places up ahead. They do it all the time for the right money." He rattled his purse with his free hand, stood, and slowly stepped away. León followed at a distance.

Estrada neared the end of the car and hesitated. Then he dodged from sight. Wind gusted and flung his panama hat back into the corridor. Just as León reached him, the author leapt from the train.

----

León hit the ground after him, tumbling and crashing through sagebrush. The impact struck the air from his lungs. Pain flared in his side, through his ribs. He clawed at the dust, trying to find his gun as the iron wheels jostled the rails, shaking the earth beneath his knees. The rumble vanished as if a wall of sound had passed over him. The train's plume of smoke hurried north.

Estrada lay, panting, clutching his jacket to protect his manuscript. León found his gun and took aim, but his hand gave such a shudder that he looked down. In his fall, he'd struck a branch that had embedded itself, just below his ribs, like an arrow.

"Put down the gun," Estrada said and sat up, his hands hanging between his knees. "I will help you. We will get a doctor. I can change your life here."

León leveled the pistol, gasping. With his free hand he pulled off the jacket and tore away his shirt. The branch was stuck deep in his side.

"It wasn't yours," León cried out, thinking that Kyros was right, that nothing could be authored, that the divine moved the pen to beauty despite the flaws of men.

"What?"

"The book. It wasn't yours."

Estrada winced. "No. Just because a man can write something beautiful does not mean that he is good. Don't confuse the two. Don't confuse the author and the man."

"Then I should have kept the book and killed you long ago. Show me the scar."

"What scar?"

"From the bullet. In the duel," León said, panting between words.

"Let me explain something," Estrada told him with a look of pity. "The book—it's not the truth. It's fiction."

"I don't understand."

León was confounded that they were discussing this now, that Estrada would lie about caring, which seemed a sacred thing, like the love in the Virgin's face.

Estrada slid his hand into his jacket to protect his manuscript.

"Listen," he told León as he moved his hand farther out of sight. "The book is a novel."

León shook his head.

"It's made up," Estrada said. "I am not that man."

As soon as he'd spoken, he jerked a gun from his jacket. But hearing his words, León had already pulled the trigger.

# ACKNOWLEDGMENTS

A book written during a period of more than twenty years presents a challenge when it comes to composing the acknowledgments. I don't remember the names of many of the people who gave me feedback on various versions of the book's many, many drafts or who provided support over the course of numerous rewrites. Among the names that I do recall are the following: Austin Lin, Bonnie Huang, Mark Preston, Heather Slomski, Corey Sobel, Nancy Romer, Lew Friedman, Dominique Fortier, Kevin Lin, Graham Moore, Arthur Moore, Nam Le, Elizabeth McKenzie, Colleen Marie Ryor, Justin Keenan, Jennifer Musi, Tristan Malavoy-Racine, Jennifer 8. Lee, Yael Goldstein Love, Greg Foster, and my mother, Bonnie Ellis. I couldn't have written "The Boy and the Lioness" without the hospitality and generosity of a number of people in Iraqi Kurdistan who shared their stories. I am grateful for the support of Canada Council for the Arts and the Writers Room in Manhattan. Special thanks to everyone at the two publishers who helped prepare this book. At Milkweed Editions: Mary Austin Speaker, Yanna Demkiewicz, Jordan Bascom, Lee Oglesby, Joey McGarvey, and Daniel Slager. At Goose Lane Editions: Susanne Alexander and Bethany Gibson.

Earlier drafts of the book's chapters appeared in the following publications: "Kali Yuga" in *Rooster*; "The Boy and the Lioness" in the *Harvard Review*; "A Song from Faraway" in *Catamaran Literary Reader*; "The Glass Ladder" in *Chicago Quarterly Review*; and "Killing the Man" in the *Adirondack Review*.

**DENI ELLIS BÉCHARD** is the author of seven previous books of fiction and nonfiction, including *Vandal Love*, winner of the 2007 Commonwealth Writers Prize, and *Into the Sun*, winner of the 2016 Midwest Book Award for Literary Fiction and selected by CBC/Radio-Canada as one of the most important books to be read by Canada's political leadership. His work has received the Nautilus Book Award for Investigative Journalism and been featured in *Best Canadian Essays*, and his photojournalism has been exhibited in the Canadian Museum of Human Rights. His articles, fiction, and photos have been published in dozens of newspapers and magazines, including the *Los Angeles Times*, *Salon*, *Reuters*, the *Paris Review*, the *Guardian*, *Patagonia*, *La Repubblica*, the *Walrus*, *Pacific Standard*, *Le Devoir*, *Vanity Fair Italia*, the *Herald* (Scotland), the *Huffington Post*, the *Harvard Review*, the *National Post*, and *Foreign Policy*. He has reported from India, Cuba, Rwanda, Colombia, Iraq, the Democratic Republic of Congo, and Afghanistan.